Rebecca's

Amish Heart Restored

THE AMISH WOMEN OF
LAWRENCE COUNTY SERIES - BOOK 2

Tracy Fredrychowski

ISBN 978-1-7371172-6-1 (paperback)

ISBN 978-1-7371172-3-0 (digital)

All Bible verses are taken from King James Version (KJV)

Published in South Carolina by The Tracer Group, LLC

https://tracyfredrychowski.com

And ye shall know the truth, and the
truth shall make you free.
John 8:32 (KJV)

By Tracy Fredrychowski

AMISH OF LAWRENCE COUNTY SERIES

Secrets of Willow Springs – Book 1

Secrets of Willow Springs – Book 2

Secrets of Willow Springs – Book 3

APPLE BLOSSOM INN SERIES

Love Blooms at the Apple Blossom Inn

NOVELLA'S

The Amish Women of Lawrence County

An Amish Gift Worth Waiting For

THE AMISH WOMEN OF LAWRENCE COUNTY

Emma's Amish Faith Tested – Book 1

Rebecca's Amish Heart Restored – Book 2

www.tracyfredrychowski.com

Contents

ABOUT THIS STORY...

While this story and its characters are figments of my imagination, Jesus Christ is very much the truth.

Throughout the United States and Canada, there are many conservative Amish orders that practice salvation through works. They believe only God can decide their eternal destiny by how well they stayed in obedience to the rules of the *Ordnung.*

Many Amish communities share traditional beliefs, much like today's Christians. However, some think the assurance of eternal salvation to be prideful and refuse to accept the truth as written in God's Word.

As I researched this story, I found that more Amish communities are moving away from their old ways. It was heart-warming to discover the truth was being taught, and they have assurance in salvation through Jesus Christ alone.

Please keep in mind not all Amish Orders are the same. And while I write the truth about finding salvation in Christ, what is practiced among the Amish may differ from community to community across the country.

A NOTE ABOUT AMISH VOCABULARY

The Amish language is called Pennsylvania Dutch and is usually spoken rather than written. The spelling of commonly used words varies from community to community throughout the United States and Canada. Even as I researched this book, some words' spelling changed within the same Amish community that inspired this story. In one case, spellings were debated between family members. Some of the terms may have slightly different spellings. Still, all come from my interactions with the Amish settlement near where I was raised in northwestern Pennsylvania.

While this book was modeled upon a small community in Lawrence County, this is a work of fiction. The names and characters are products of my imagination. They do not resemble any person, living or dead, or actual events in that community.

LIST OF CHARACTERS

Rebecca Byler. Prideful twenty-four-year-old Amish woman and daughter to newly appointed minister Jacob Byler.

Eli Bricker. Neighbor to the Byler's and past love interest to Rebecca.

Mary Bricker. Eli's old ailing grandmother.

Andy Bricker. Eli's father and Mary's sixty-three-year-old son, from Lancaster, Pennsylvania.

Anna Byler. Rebecca's twin sister.

Emma Yoder. Rebecca and Anna's younger sister and wife to Samuel.

Samuel Yoder. The source of some of Rebecca's hostility toward Emma.

Jacob Byler. Minister and father to Rebecca, Anna, and Emma.

Wilma Byler. Jacob's new wife from neighboring Willow Brook.

Bishop Weaver. A church leader in Willow Springs.

Tracy Fredrychowski

MAP OF WILLOW SPRINGS

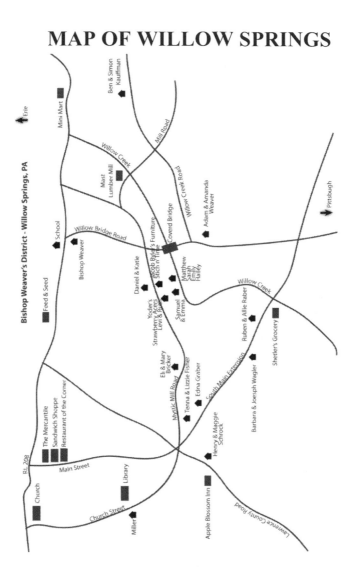

ix

PROLOGUE

May - Willow Springs, Pennsylvania

The rhythmic movement of Rebecca Byler's spinning wheel picked up speed as she thought about her run-in with her younger *schwester*, Emma. In all her twenty-three years, she'd never been more aggravated than she was at that moment. When the roving of alpaca fiber she let slide through her thumb and index finger hit a clump of dark matter, she pulled back and let the draft of yarn fall to the floor. "Ugh! I don't have time for this."

Rebecca's twin, Anna, stopped the drum roller and turned her way. "Now what?"

"I'm still finding bits of hay in the roving. You're not getting it clean enough."

Anna stooped down and picked up the tan cloud of fiber and held it toward the light of the window. "I don't see anything."

"I felt it. Look closer."

Anna held it out. "I don't see a thing; show me."

Rebecca waved her off. "Just be more careful when you're picking and carding. We can't afford to have our customers complain our yarn isn't clean enough."

Anna threw the clump back in the carding box and asked, "What's got you all worked up today?"

Irritation crept up Rebecca's neck as she replayed the argument that she had at the bakery earlier that morning. "Can you believe Emma had the nerve to tell me I was hateful?"

"Why did she say that?"

"Things would be so much better around here if she would've stayed in Sugarcreek."

Anna tilted her head. "I bet you provoked her. It doesn't sound like something Emma would say."

Rebecca snarled, "Why do you always insist on taking her side?"

"I'm not taking anyone's side, but I know how you get."

"What's that supposed to mean?"

"You tell me. You've been harping on Emma for months and nit-picking about every little thing. If you don't watch it, word is going to get back to *datt,* and then you'll really have something to fuss about."

"Me? It's Emma who should be worried. I don't know what she and Samuel are up to, but they've got something they're hiding, and I'll figure it out one way or another."

"Rebecca, why are you so set on causing them trouble?"

"She's the one who thinks she's better than everyone else."

"How do you figure?"

"Think about it. First, she runs off to Sugarcreek to spend time with her birth family and leaves *Mamm* when she needed her most. In my books, *Mamm* would still be alive if she hadn't spent the last few months of her life worrying about Emma. Next, she strings Samuel along for months only to come back assuming he'd drop everything and take her back."

Anna laid a cloud of fiber in front of the teeth of the drum. She turned the handle to feed the batt through, combing it in long, smooth batches. "Why are you harping on this? That was three years ago."

"Because it was the start of her prancing around like we all owe her something."

"You're exaggerating. Emma doesn't act like that at all. You don't give her enough credit. How do you think you would have felt if you found out *Mamm* and *Datt* weren't really your parents after sixteen years?"

Rebecca snarled, "Elated that she wasn't really my *schwester*!"

Anna gasped. "You take that back. You don't really mean it."

"I won't, and I do."

"You are hateful, and I can see why Emma said that to you. You best take your attitude to the Lord before it gets you in trouble."

The bell above the door to their father's shop jingled, and Rebecca snapped, "I'll get it."

Their father built a room off the side of his furniture shop for them to sell the yarn they produced from the alpacas raised on their farm. A divider kept the washing, sorting, and spinning area separate from the display floor and the customers. In the two years since they'd opened their store, *Stitch 'n Time,* their alpaca and specialty wool yarns had become a popular stop for both the Amish and English. They even started offering hand-made products, on consignment, from the women in their community.

Rebecca made her way around two spinning wheels and pulled the curtain aside to step out into the store. Their father had built display racks along the outside wall to hold the hand-dyed fiber. An array of baskets sat on the worktable in the middle of the room that contained mittens, hats, socks, and scarves available for sale. Canisters of different sized crochet hooks and knitting needles adorned the counter by the cash register.

It didn't take her but a second to recognize Samuel's broad shoulders and wisps of hair that flipped up from behind his straw hat. "Samuel?"

He turned toward her and in an irritated tone, stated, "I'd like a word with you."

"What about?"

"Let's step outside."

Her lip turned upward before saying, "The porch? Not so sure that would be the honorable thing to do with your wife's *schwester*."

"I'm in no mood for your shenanigans," he moved her way and whispered, "I can air your dirty laundry right here so Anna and your *datt* can hear, or we can take this outside."

She moved to the door and to the far end of the porch. "So, what is so important that we had to come out here?"

"We can start with your visit to the bakery this morning. Don't you think Emma's had enough to deal with the last six months? She doesn't need your verbal abuse to add to it."

Rebecca crossed her arms over her chest. "I only spoke the truth."

"I don't believe a word that comes from your mouth. It wouldn't be the first time you've stirred up trouble for your own benefit."

She snapped her head in his direction. "Like I've said before, if you bring any of that back up, I'll tell your sweet little Emma exactly how her wonder boy behaved while she was away."

He moved closer and snarled, "Don't threaten me."

She backed up. "*Ohhh* ...did I hit a nerve?"

"Don't think for a minute that I'll stand by and watch you harass my wife. Whatever you think she's done is no concern of yours, and I'll warn you one last time. Keep your snide remarks and accusations to yourself."

"Or what? You'll tell whom, the bishop?"

"I mean it, Rebecca, don't go there."

Rebecca walked back to the door, held her hand on the knob, and said, "The way I see it, you have a lot more to lose than I do."

He walked toward her, stopped at her shoulder, and muttered in her ear. "That's where you're wrong. I've already made my peace with God ...have you?"

She snapped back. "But have you made your peace with my *schwester*?"

He didn't respond to her question but walked off the porch and into his waiting buggy.

Her nails dug into the palm of her hand, and she clenched her teeth at his comment. She'd kept his secret for years, holding onto it until just the right time when it could cause the most pain. If he thought for one minute that, she wouldn't use it to get her revenge, then he was sadly mistaken. If she planned it right, her little *schwester* would be sorry she ever stepped foot back in Willow Springs.

CHAPTER 1

Through the shop window Rebecca could see Wilma hanging clothes. Just the sight of her stepmother unleashed a series of not so flattering thoughts.

For the life of me, I don't see what Datt sees in that woman. She's as dreary as an early spring sky. For certain, he only married her for fear Anna and I would leave him to fend for himself. I'm not sure why men think they have to have a woman around to take care of them. I, for one, don't ever plan on getting married, and God forbid a man thinks he has the right to tell me what to do, and how or what I should be thinking. I won't have it, that's for sure, Amish or not.

I learned soon after Mamm died that I couldn't count on anyone but myself. I've even put myself out there a time or two and let a few boys give me a ride home from a singeon. But they are all the same. They want their wives to be some milly-mouse, yes-sir, shell of a human being. Even Emma has become that to Samuel. I can see how she follows him around and tends to his every need.

I must admit there are days I see Mamm in Emma more so than in either Anna or me. As much as I hate to admit it, even though Emma is not my biological schwester, Emma favors Mamm's mannerisms more than I do. I sure do miss mamm's sweet disposition, even though I tested it more than once growing up.

Datt's new wife, of just six months is nothing like my mamm. She's brassy and a tad bit bossy, and I fail to understand why he married the old spinster in the first place.

With no children of her own, she's taken to telling Datt how to deal with Anna and me. She has no right, that's for sure and certain. If I'd known his Sunday afternoon visits to Willow Brook, ten miles north of Willow Springs, would produce a stepmother, I would have kept his mind occupied on things that really mattered. Perhaps I should have done more to convince him my yarn business needed to include a kiosk at the Grove City Mall.

As it stands, Wilma has made it clear that no young woman should have thoughts of growing a business when her mind should be concentrating on securing a husband and raising babies. She thinks business should be left to the head of the household, and no talk of such things should be left to a woman. What does Wilma know anyway? It's not like she ever did either of those things in her fifty-five years on this earth.

Just the thought of her adding her two cents makes my skin crawl. I guess it's best I spend all my time here in the store and let her have the run of the house like she wants. If anything, it helps Anna's anxiety if I keep my mouth shut and my opinions to myself.

To be quite honest, I couldn't care less about what Wilma thinks. The only thing that matters is that I protect my twin. I might only be minutes older than Anna, but she's not as strong-willed as me and gets frazzled quickly. It's been almost five years since Mamm passed, and Anna continues to battle with anxiety over the smallest things. Anything out of the normal will send her into a bout of heart palpitations and stomach pains.

Datt and Wilma are trying to force her into facing her fears, but I know my schwester best. Anna needs to let me continue to shelter her like I always have. We've worked things out; why can't they just leave things alone.

"Isn't that right, *schwester*?"

Anna pulled the curtain aside that kept her shielded from the customers in the front of the yarn shop. "Were you talking to me?"

"Not so much you, but myself. I was just thinking that *Datt* and Wilma don't need to butt their noses into our arrangements. We have everything worked out between the two of us, and it's none of their business how we manage the shop."

Anna stood and carried an armful of yarn to the display rack beside the front counter. "Well, to be quite honest, as long as our shop is inside of *Datt's* furniture store, and we still live under his roof, I'd say he still has some say in the matter."

Anna's bold statement made heat fill Rebecca's face and retreat in the wake of cold frustration. "But we've worked hard making this shop what it is today. *Datt* didn't help us with that. We did it on our own. It was us shearing the alpacas, and it was us working day and night creating the right natural dyes that have made the shop so successful."

Anna replied, pointing to an array of pink and purple skeins in a basket on the counter. "I do love how we figured out beetroot and the right amount of vinegar would result in this beautiful dark pink."

"See, that was us, not *Datt*. He didn't spend hours boiling goldenrod, pokeberry, and black walnuts until his hands and fingernails were stained beyond recognition."

Rebecca bounced a pencil on the counter and Anna quickly laid her hand over it before saying, "No, he didn't. But he did build us this shop and provide the financial support to get it off the ground. In my books, he has every right to tell us how and what we should be doing."

Rebecca snatched her hand from Anna's grasp. "Not you too! Here I am trying to protect you, and you're turning on me."

"Oh, *schwester,* I'm not turning on you; I'm only trying to get you to see *Datt* has our best interest in mind. I don't even know what's got you so worked up this morning."

"Wilma, that's what. She prances into our life and thinks she knows what's best for us. We were doing just fine on our own all these years. Why did *Datt* have to go and upset the apple cart?"

"Rebecca, come on, can't you see he's changed since Wilma came to live with us? He's much happier. He's not nearly as short with us, and not once since he sat us all down to warn us about his new position as minister, has he taken on such a harsh tone. I contribute that to Wilma.

I can see he's finally found his way back to the man we knew long before *Mamm* passed and long before we found out Emma had another family other than our own. How can you fault him for finding happiness in someone other than his children?"

Rebecca walked back to the window and thought. *I don't have to like it, and I'm not about to back down without a fight.* She'd poured her heart and soul into *Stitch 'n Time* and wasn't about to let her stepmother have any say in how she ran it.

Turning from the window, Rebecca straightened a basket of patterns and said, "I should have known you'd side with her. Your quest to be peacemaker grates on my nerves to a point I don't even want to discuss things with you. Did you know she told *Datt* it wasn't a woman's place to make business decisions?"

"What decision is that?"

"I want to expand our business to the mall, but Wilma butted in and convinced *Datt* I should be looking for a husband instead. She even went as far as telling me that I need to let you help the customers more. They think I coddle you too much."

Anna tucked a loose strand of chestnut brown hair under her *kapp*. "I certainly appreciate you taking on that role, but you aren't doing either one of us any good stewing about everything that comes out of Wilma's mouth." Anna picked up a bucket of clean fiber and headed back to the spinning wheel concealed by the heavy curtain that kept her hidden from the public.

Rebecca sat on the stool near the counter and rested her head in her hands. She rubbed both of her temples and thought. *I can't think about Wilma right now. I have to find a way to support myself.*

If living under her parent's roof meant she didn't have a say in the outcome of her life, she would need to find a way to branch out on her own. Her idea of selling their all-natural dyed and handspun yarn at the mall was the perfect solution. Even if it meant she would have to go against her Amish upbringing and decline the prospect of marriage in place of her independence. Wasn't it God who said singleness was a gift? If it was good enough for Jesus, why couldn't it be good enough for her? Besides, being single would allow her time to devote more of herself to God. *That's perfect ... I'll tell that to Datt and Wilma. How can they chastise me for wanting to serve God and the community?*

Rebecca pulled out a stack of receipts and entered them in the ledger with a new plan in place.

***

Anna set the table as Wilma and her father spoke in hushed whispers in the front room. She passed Eli Bricker, their neighbor, on her way into the house. He tipped his hat her way but didn't speak a word. Wondering if something had happened to his grandmother, Mary, she strained to hear what her parents talked about. It was announced at church a month ago the elderly woman suffered a stroke. The last she heard; Mary was in a rehabilitation hospital in Mercer.

Wilma removed the lid from the pot simmering on the stove and asked, "Is Rebecca on her way in?"

Anna started to slice a loaf of fresh bread that was cooling on the counter. "I believe so. She was just about done washing a batch of fiber and said she'd be in as soon as she hung it to dry."

"Your father and I have some things we want to discuss with you before you head back out to the shop."

Anna took a deep breath, taking in the savory aroma of chicken stew. "Oh, that smells good!" She broke off a piece of bread and dipped it in the thick gravy.

Wilma batted her hand away, but not before she plopped the bread in her mouth. "I swear, for such a little thing, you sure do have an appetite."

Anna wiped her mouth with the back of her hand and went back to slicing bread. "I saw Eli leave. Did he mention how Mary was doing?"

"That's what we want to talk to you girls about. Let's wait for your father and Rebecca."

Anna lost herself in her own thoughts as she finished with the bread. There was a time when she thought Rebecca and Eli might be courting, but that was short-lived and long before their *mamm* passed away and Emma married Samuel. With all of them being around the same age, she wasn't sure if Eli attended *singeons* any longer. While twenty-four was anything but old, neither Rebecca, Eli, nor herself went out of their way to find a mate. One thing was for sure, she was happy Eli was there to take care of Mary.

Mary Bricker was one of the sweetest women she knew. Her husband died five years ago, and when he did, Eli left his father's home in Lancaster and moved to Willow Springs to care for his grandmother. That spoke mountains of truth into Eli's character. She wondered why Rebecca or any other young girl in Lawrence County hadn't noticed.

***

Jacob took his place at the head of the table and waited until Wilma and his daughters sat before bowing his head. Clearing his throat to signal prayer was over, he handed his bowl to his wife and said, "Eli stopped by earlier to tell us he brought Mary home the other day. He needs a nursemaid to assist her with some womanly things he's not comfortable doing."

Anna spoke up. "I would be more than happy to help. I'm sure Eli couldn't help her bathe and such."

Jacob took his filled bowl back from Wilma and turned to respond to Anna. "While I'm pleased, you're so willing to help our neighbor in need, I think I'd like Rebecca to go instead."

Rebecca stopped her spoon in mid-air as a wince of disappointment flashed across Anna's face. Without thinking of the consequences, words flew from Rebecca's lips. "What would make you consider anything so utterly ridiculous?" A hush filled the room as Anna and Wilma held their breath. The vein at Jacob's temple pulsed, and he wiped his mouth with a napkin before responding.

"Exactly why you'll be the one tending to Mary Bricker. Your lack of compassion to see past your own needs is something I've warned you about. It's high time you put your own selfish desires to rest and think about someone else for a change."

Her tone was grated. "But what about the yarn shop?"

Rebecca was positively trembling. Just when she thought she had everything planned out, *Datt* upset the apple cart again.

Without letting her father even answer, she continued, "Anna isn't comfortable helping the customers like I am. I think I would be better suited to care for the shop than Mary."

Jacob dipped his bread in his bowl. "My decision is final. You will help Eli with Mary starting tomorrow."

Rebecca's heart pounded in anger as she thought. *Doesn't anyone in this family have a bit of common sense? Sending me to help an old woman will end in disaster, I'm sure of it.*

***

Tears welled up in Anna's eyes, but she refused to let them drop at the table, let alone in front of her family. Rebecca was correct in saying she wasn't comfortable dealing with the customers. The mere thought of talking to strangers sent her into a panic attack. Why couldn't *Datt* see her *schwester* was better suited to run the shop.

Rebecca left the table and slammed the front door, leaving Anna to face her father alone. In not much more than a whisper, she stated, "*Datt*, I really wouldn't mind helping Mary. I'd much prefer that than running the shop."

In a soothing tone, he replied, "I know, but you need to trust me on this one. I know what's right for both of my daughters. Someday you'll thank me."

Anna rose slowly and cleared the table, her head down. Her eyes burned at the cruel irony. The dream she never told anyone was within reach, all to be snatched away. Tending to her own mother's illness awoke a deep-rooted desire to be a nurse. Even the agonizing thoughts of dealing with people was overshadowed by her desire to give comfort to the sick. All she could hope for in her Amish community, who didn't believe in higher education, was serving her community as a nursemaid. Yet again, she was thrown into situations that tested her anxiety levels, much like running the yarn shop. That was Rebecca's vision, not hers.

Trembling again, she leaned back against the kitchen counter, reeling herself through the disappointment.

***

Rebecca clenched her teeth as she made her way back to the yarn shop. There was no reasoning with her father, and she was sure Wilma put him up to this. Since when did either of them believe she had the patience to care for an old lady? Let alone spend time with Eli Bricker. That time had long passed. He was the one that said her tongue was a bit too sharp for his liking. Whatever that meant. Now she was being forced to take care of his grandmother. This is not what she had planned, and she'd have to find a way to put a stop to it and fast. It was time she started making her own decisions, one way or another. Inhaling through her nose, she released her breath slowly to calm herself. Like a wave of fog on a chilly spring morning, old resentments started to simmer as the past flooded her mind.

Sitting behind the spinning wheel, she coiled fiber between her fingers and started to pump the treadle that spun the soft fleece around the bobbin. Speaking as if there was someone in the shop to answer, she asked, "Why God? I've prayed and prayed, but still, you don't answer my prayers. I attend church regularly; I've committed myself to the *Ordnung,* I drop things in the sunshine box whenever I can, and I even go as far as attending work frolics even though I hate them. What more do I have to do to get what I want?"

Rebecca frowned in annoyance, thinking about all she'd done to gain God's favor despite the sin surrounding her past.

With a sense of conviction, she heard the following words echo between her ears *…you can start with honoring your father.*

There wasn't an ounce of breath she was going to breathe into the fleeting words that left her head as quickly as they entered.

Lord, I see no way out of this. What should I do?

***

After a day of listening to Rebecca voice her complaints and a supper of utter silence, Anna sat cross-legged in the middle of her bed, clutching a pillow against her chest. Why did Rebecca always make things so complicated?

Oh, God, you know how much I want to follow you and never want to second guess your plans. But just once, I'd like Rebecca to see what she does to this family. I've tried to understand her, really, I have. Please help her see it doesn't always have to be about her.

Anna whispered to herself. "Does loving your neighbor as yourself always mean you have to give up on your dreams for the sake of living out someone else's?"

The last thing Anna wanted to do was let bitterness toward her *schwester* fester too deep, but she was so frustrated. For once, couldn't Rebecca just do what she was asked without making life miserable for everyone around her?

Anna wanted to love her *schwester* as God instructed her to do, but it was getting harder and harder. After the day they had, she could barely endure the thoughts of spending another evening listening to Rebecca. Like always, her thoughts were tucked deep inside in hopes of extinguishing any fire her words might ignite. Hopefully, she'd be fast asleep before Rebecca came to bed.

***

If Rebecca Byler was good at one thing, it was holding grudges. She kept a list of grievances against every hurt she'd ever suffered, regardless of who caused it. She never forgot, and God forbid if she forgave quickly. The past was like the ledger in her shop, offenses were deposited often, and withdraws came few and far between.

Much like Samuel's sharp words engraved so deep in her soul, she still remembered them word for word, as if it were yesterday.

"Rebecca Byler, there's going to come a time when your self-centeredness is going to cause you great harm. Always thinking about yourself with no regard for how your actions may affect someone else is going to keep you away from God."

She didn't remember the molten words she poured back at him, but she recalled what happened next. The night that would forever be etched in her memory and one she was sure kept God from hearing her prayers.

CHAPTER 2

Mary Bricker took a few labored steps from the table to the kitchen sink. Her entire right side was limp from a stroke she suffered four weeks earlier. She leaned into the quad stick and dragged her right foot until she could steady her poor balance at the counter.

The house sat quiet, and only the wall clock bonged softly from the living room. Eli headed to the barn hours ago and she yearned to open the window above the sink. The sun was just making its way above the horizon, and the sky was filled with pinks and yellows, welcoming the spring day into view. Though her home was closed up tight, she could faintly hear the cooing of a pair of mourning doves outside the window.

Loving the sounds of springtime and the smell of the hyacinths planted below the window, she longed to let God's beauty fill the air. Pushing her hip into the counter and reclaiming her posture with her good hand, she looked at her gnarled hand and gave up hope. Instead, she stared out over the kitchen garden. Normally, Eli would have already plowed and tended to the soil. Leaving her to plant the tender spring lettuce and early radishes that would adorn their dinner table for weeks.

Other than some arthritis settling in her knees, she felt spry and full of life before the stroke. Even after her husband died five years earlier, she didn't stop enjoying life. Her grandson, Eli, coming to live with her only added more joy to her home. Her outwardly bubbly personality suffered only after the unexpected decline in her health. Now all she could think of was how she had become a burden to Eli. Sadness filled her, and loneliness deepened with each passing day.

Eli was young and ill-prepared to take care of his aging grandmother. His unease at helping her with womanly things became apparent when she soiled herself and needed his help. While he was patient and kind, his posture spoke a million words of discomfort. He was just twenty-four and without any *schwesters* of his own, he was ill-equipped to tend to her more personal needs.

Making her way back to her chair, she rubbed her hand over the well-used oak table that had been a wedding present from her husband, Noah. Their marriage, one of convenience, grew into a sweet reminder of God's undying provisions. The life they lived in Willow Springs glorified God in every way imaginable, even after an unspeakable sin sealed their fate.

The quietness was almost deafening as her mind drifted to those troubled times when their one and only child, Andy, left Willow Springs to live with his grandfather in Lancaster. The pain and brokenness stayed planted on her husband's face for years. They vowed they wouldn't share their secret with Andy; the pain of his betrayal was still too raw to verbalize. However, Mary felt an overwhelming desire to share their story with Andy. He had to know the truth before it was buried deep in the grave beside her.

Eli, unlike his father, didn't idolize their family's heritage and would be quick to defend one ill-spoken word against herself or Noah. Her husband's final words spoken on his death bed still rang in her ears, as clear as his undying love for her.

"You've been good to my family, Mary."

Though not always easy, Mary learned early on that she mustn't harbor any unresolved bitterness or unconfessed sin if she wanted to hear from the Lord. She had long forgiven her husband's family and spent her life upholding the name of God to all those around her.

Resentment stayed rooted in Andy's heart, so much that he refused to attend his own father's funeral. Mary blinked, hurt lodged deep in the back of her throat.

Oh Lord, will Andy even care when I'm gone? Will he shed a single tear? What more could I have done? I love my son as you do; how can I make him see what sacrifice his father made for him?

For years, she tried to keep her family together and failed in all attempts to reunite her son with his father.

Tears bristled Mary's eyes, blurring her vision. Her heart ached. Andy was always too busy to write, too busy to visit, just too busy to fulfill a dying man's wish.

Rubbing the knuckles on her useless hand, she winced in pain as she stretched her arthritis-filled knee straight.

From where she sat, she could view her long-abandoned flower garden through the picture window at the back of the kitchen.

The ache in her heart matched the tangled rose vines and unkempt bushes. Once a place of renewal, the shaggy garden was overrun with patches of dandelions and dead seed pods. Empty pots sat, still filled with soil, and were waiting for a new life springtime had always promised.

For years, Noah and she shared a love of gardening. They spent countless hours combing through an array of seed catalogs that would arrive every January like clockwork. Oh, how much fun they had sketching out new garden beds and planning new color themes. Now the stack of beautiful glossy pages sat untouched in a basket near her late husband's chair. Much like their life, awaiting the first signs of life after a long Northwestern Pennsylvania winter.

Stretching her fingers slowly, Mary reached for the Budget newspaper. The scribes shared snippets of life much like that in Willow Springs, a constant reminder of how life went on. She often found herself looking forward to the weekly subscription. Still, since her weakened stance prohibited her from holding the pages upright, the strain of reading the words was tiresome.

An unfamiliar grumpiness took over, and she pushed the paper aside and mumbled, "It's the same old stuff week after week. Why would I want to read it anyway?"

Lord, look at me. I've become a cranky old woman, reminiscing about things I have no control over. Why don't you just take me home now?

The nurses at the rehab center told her she should exercise her mind as much as her body, and she reached for the crossword puzzle book. The last thing she needed to put on Eli's already full shoulders was a bad case of Alzheimer's. Heaven help her if she wandered outside without any clothes on, and Eli had to cover her.

She pulled the book closer with her strong hand and struggled to hold the pen. She lifted her weak arm and used it as a paperweight on the flimsy pages. Even if she knew the answer to the puzzle, her left hand would prove useless in writing legible letters. In a fit of frustration, she pushed the book aside, making it land on the floor as the pen rolled under the stove.

Tears burned Mary's eyes as she stared down at the book. Unable to retrieve it, she laid her head on the table, letting defeat and grief envelop her. Unable to think of anything else, she lost herself in thoughts of Andy's betrayal. Would he have acted the same if they'd told him the truth? Look what the secret had cost them and what burden it put upon Eli.

I kept our secret, my darling, just as you asked. But it's time Andy knows the truth about his grandfather. Please forgive me, but it's the only way I see to let Eli live the life he so deserves. Andy must step up and assume responsibility to me in my weakened state.

She clung to hope as Eli's heavy boots stomped off layers of mud before opening the door.

"*Mommi*, what are you doing at the table? Let me help you back to your chair in the front room."

Mary lifted her head and wiped the moisture from the corners of her eyes. "I wanted to hear the birds and smell the flowers."

"You can do that from the living room. I'll open the front window for you."

Mary leaned into Eli's firm grip as he guided her back to the rocker near the window. "You are a good boy, Eli, and I'm not sure what I would have done had you not been here to look after me."

"Now, *Mommi,* don't go getting all sentimental on me. I'm only doing what any good grandson would do for his favorite grandmother."

"I'm your only grandmother, if I'm not mistaken."

"And that makes you my favorite."

Eli tucked a lap blanket around her legs and unleashed the window sash to let in the early spring breeze.

"I stopped by Jacob Byler's this morning, and he's agreed to send one of the twins by to help you get ready for the day."

"Did you let him know I prefer Rebecca over Anna?"

"I did, even though I'm not sure why you would choose Rebecca. I would think Anna would be more compatible with you than Rebecca."

"If you remember, I quite enjoyed Rebecca's company until, for some unknown reason, she stopped coming by."

Eli's face took on a flash of color that changed the temperature in the room as quickly as a wildfire.

Mary looked up at her grandson's lofty stature and asked. "Whatever happened between the two of you?"

"I can't remember what day it is, let alone what happened five years ago."

Mary smiled at his outright lie. There was no doubt by the way he refused to look her in the eye that he was putting her off for his own protection.

"Now, how about I make you a cup of tea before I head back outside? I have two ewes about ready to lamb."

Mary smoothed out the quilt on her lap. "Maybe Rebecca can help you when she comes tomorrow. I won't need her by my side all day. Besides, if she's going to buy the wool from shearing this year, she might want to see what it takes to raise sheep."

Eli patted his grandmother's shoulder. "Oh no, you don't. You're not sticking her on me. You're the one who wanted her over Anna. She can stay right here in the house out of my way. The last thing I want is a know-it-all woman telling me how to tend my flock."

Mary snickered. "Looks like I touched a sore spot."

Eli picked his hat up from the chair and headed back to the kitchen, contemplating his grandmother's words.

The sounds of Eli making tea instantly faded as Mary lovingly stared at her husband's chair. For weeks after his death, the only comfort she found was when she sank down in it. His smell lingered on the blanket thrown over the back, and the well-worn wooden arms soothed her. When she closed her eyes, she could feel his warmth surround her. Over time, the smell faded, and eventually, she made new chair covers and replaced the tattered lap blanket with a new one.

Now, in the light of a new day, she had become him. Sitting, staring, and waiting for her time to pass. They talked little in those final months of his life, but no words could fill their already full life. They were blessed beyond belief, and they had no regrets. Well, she thought so anyway. That was until Eli gave up his life to take care of hers. One that he could get back. If only she could shed light on the darkness of a secret she swore to never tell.

Lord, what's the point? Maybe it would be better if I got Alzheimer's. Then I wouldn't realize my only son refuses to acknowledge me. What if I did forget everything? Wouldn't that be better than the sting of his rejection?

Mary pressed her lips together and let the sweet smell of spring flutter across her nose.

***

The heat continued to warm Eli's cheeks long after escaping his grandmother's questions. His short-lived courtship with Rebecca Byler left a sour taste in his mouth that forced him to give up all hopes of finding a woman to share his life with. He always thought he was a good judge of character, but Rebecca

34

proved him wrong. From catching her in a compromising situation to trying to curb her overpowering personality, he'd given up on all women. Especially when he'd lost his heart to the chestnut brown-haired, green-eyed beauty.

Even the thought of Rebecca spending time on his farm made anger bloom deep in his belly. It was one thing to see her at church or tip his hat at her passing buggy, but here in his kitchen, sharing a meal was going a bit too far for his liking.

Maybe he needed to try calling his father one more time. Mary's care was too much for him to handle on his own, but the thought of listening to his father give one more excuse as to why he or his mother couldn't be bothered left him restless. Didn't they realize she was fading fast, and soon the brightness in her eyes would fade for good? Not for one minute did he want to believe the explanations they hurled at him.

For years, his parent's tone changed to muted mumbles anytime his grandparents' names were mentioned. He never understood the distance between them, but after his grandfather died, he took it upon himself to come look after the farm. Totally against the wishes of his own parents, and in time, the distance he recognized as he was growing up extended to include him. His younger *bruders* took up the slack on his father's dairy farm, and his absence was barely noticed within months.

His grandmother, on the other hand, was gracious and loving and provided him with the most God-centered home he'd ever experienced. It was under her loving guidance that he came to discover the truth of Jesus, even though their Old-Order community failed to teach them the complete truth. In the wee hours of the morning, long before he headed to the barn to care for the sheep, they studied God's word in secret.

He'd long given up hope Rebecca could be the wife he longed for. The seasons came and passed, one merging into another until time stood still in that exact moment.

Steam escaped through the small holes in the teakettle, whistling a tune as his thoughts drifted back to the present. Bouncing a tea bag up and down in the hot liquid, the bold black tea scent filled his nose as he carried the cup to the front room.

"Here you go *Mommi*, this should hold you over until I come in for dinner. Do you need anything?"

Mary's eyelids brimmed with tears, and she looked toward the bathroom. The chair toilet Eli carried in from the barn sat to her left. He lifted the chair and placed it inside the small room without saying anything. Easing her anxiousness, he put her quad stick in her left hand and guided her toward the door.

Mary felt the warmth before Eli noticed the puddle on the floor. She gasped and whispered through broken gurgles. "I'm sorry you have to deal with this again."

"It's my job to take care of you, and that's exactly what I plan on doing."

"But cleaning up an old woman is not in your job title."

"And taking in your grandson wasn't in your job title either, but you did it anyway."

Once in the bathroom, Eli wrapped a strong arm around her waist, pulled her skirt up, and turned his head as she struggled to pull her soiled undergarments out from underneath the long, dark fabric. Once they fell past her knees, he helped her sit. It took every ounce of control Mary had to keep the situation dignified. In a manner, much like his personality, he lovingly prepared a warm washcloth, laid it on the counter close to her, and picked up the soiled underwear off the floor. Tears teetered and toppled over her lashes as she lost so much of her life.

***

Filling the bucket at the sink, Eli reminisced about the times his grandmother cared for him over the years. Why she felt she had become a burden to him was beyond him. The look etched on her face spoke of broken dreams and shattered independence. Maybe she was right in forcing him to hire Rebecca. Perhaps she wouldn't feel so embarrassed with a woman looking after her personal needs. He needed to get out of his own head and put aside his reservations about Rebecca being underfoot and doing what was best for his grandmother. But could Rebecca be trusted with the one person that meant more to him than life itself?

After throwing the water out, he hung the mop on the hook and waited for his grandmother to call his name.

In not much more than a whisper, he heard, "Eli, are you still in the house?"

He walked to the door. "I am. Are you finished?"

"I need clean undergarments. Can you fetch them for me?"

Without answering, he moved to her room and retrieved what she required before opening the bathroom door.

"Do you need my help?"

Biting her bottom lip, Mary nodded and took in a deep breath to calm herself.

Eli placed her feet in each leg opening and pulled them up to her knees. In one swift movement, he pulled her to her feet, held her skirt up, and turned his head while she maneuvered her undergarment in place. Her frail body quivered in his arms, and without asking permission, he slid his arms under her knees and carried her to the bedroom.

No words were shared as he tucked her beneath a quilt and kissed her forehead before he left.

Eli softly shut the door, slipped back in his boots, and headed to the barn. The herd of sheep waiting to be fed could go on about their day with little knowledge of his presence. Still, his grandmother would be a constant reminder of what God's steadfast love meant to another human being. Mary was his life, and he wasn't sure he could trust her wellbeing to just anyone, especially Rebecca Byler.

CHAPTER 3

Rebecca walked to the Bricker house, irritated and tense. The ten minutes it took her to walk up Mystic Mill Road, Eli's Hill, as many called it, did little to calm her racing pulse. There was no changing her father's mind even after she pleaded with him during breakfast.

Taking in the early morning chill, she filled her lungs and hoped she wouldn't have to run into Eli. If only her father knew Eli couldn't stand the sight of her, he might have allowed Anna to come instead. But that would require her to explain their sordid past, which was nobody's business but her own.

Mouth tight, Rebecca knocked on the front door. While she waited, she took note of the overgrown rose bushes near the porch and the weeds that covered the kitchen garden. There was a time when the Bricker house was well-cared for, but by the looks of it, Eli had bitten off more than he could chew with Mary's stroke. A pair of rockers sat on the far end of the porch, and she recalled Mary and her late husband spending many evenings there. Two hanging pots hung above the railing, connected by a giant garden spider. The flowerpots contained last summer's ferns, now brown and scraggly.

Rebecca knocked on the door again and moved to the front window. The panes of glass needed a good washing, and she used her finger to wipe a spot away to peek inside. The living room sat empty.

"I believe I hired a nursemaid, not a peeping tom."

Suddenly agitated, Rebecca turned toward Eli's voice. "I knocked on the door a couple of times, and when no one answered, I wanted to make sure Mary was okay."

Eli opened the door and motioned her to follow him inside. "I'm pretty sure she's sleeping. She had a rough morning, and I helped her back to bed before I went to the barn."

Rebecca hung her sweater on the peg by the door and wiped her black sneakers on the rug. She tried not to look around and judge Eli's cleaning abilities, but by the grime on the floor and the clutter in the corner, she could tell he kept his work to the outside of the house only. In an instant, heat rose inside of

Rebecca like steam from a teapot. *If he thought she'd be doing more than tending to Mary's personal needs for one minute, he had another thing coming. She was a lot of things, but a maid wasn't one of them.*

Eli looked aghast as she clicked her tongue at the pile of dirty dishes on the counter.

"For one thing, you can get that look off your face. I do the best I can, but it's spring, and I have lambs popping out left and right around here. The last thing I have time for is a stack of dirty dishes. I'll get to them later. For now, all I care to talk about is my grandmother's care."

Rebecca threw her hands up. "I didn't say a word, now did I?"

"You didn't have to. It was written all over your face."

Rebecca saw a hint of annoyance in his blue-green eyes. For a swift moment, his cheeks took on the color of the red onion skinned dye she made for her latest batch of fiber. Forcing herself to turn her face from his, she moved a stack of newspapers off a chair and sat down.

"How about you tell me what your expectations are, and I'll tell you if they match mine."

Eli crossed his arms over his chest and leaned back on the counter. "Excuse me. I do believe I'm paying you. So, it's you who must live up to my expectations, not the other way around."

Rebecca crossed her legs and bounced her foot up and down. She didn't like being reprimanded, especially by Eli Bricker. Too much water had passed under their bridge for her to tolerate his arrogance.

"Whatever! Just tell me what you want me to do."

Eli paused long enough to let the sting of her words settle. "Look, for some reason, my grandmother insisted you be the one to take care of her. So, no matter what we think of each other, we need to make this work for her. All I care about is that she is fed, happy, and well cared for – understood?"

The lines on Rebecca's forehead magnified. "Why would she want me and not Anna?"

"I have no idea. But as you know, she has a mind of her own, and there's no changing it."

Rebecca lifted her chin and stared him straight in the eye. He might tower over her, but she needed to set a few things straight right from the start. "I'm here only because my father gave me no other option, but I'm here against my will. I will take care of Mary and Mary alone. I won't be washing your clothes or cleaning up after you. As for your meals, if I make enough, you are more than welcome to clean up Mary's leftovers, but other than that, I'm here only to take care of her. Understood?"

He opened his mouth, but she didn't give him the chance to respond.

"Either that works for you, or I go back and tell my father you fired me."

Pressing his lips together, he headed to the door, reached for the doorknob, and stopped and turned her way. "I do believe you told me once that I was the rudest boy you'd ever met. Well, guess what? You're the meanest spirited woman I've ever known, and I can see five years did nothing to curb your ugly disposition."

Rebecca's stomach flipped as she remembered the exact moment she told him that. It was the first time he'd shown any interest in her. And it was at the same time he told her that a girl as pretty as her should wear more smiles. She'd never admit it to anyone, but a part of her missed the carefree days of her youth and the way Eli Bricker used to look at her. But that was long before secrets and accusations clouded her heart, much like the film covering the yellowed linoleum under her feet.

"Maybe you're just as much to blame. If I remember correctly, you once told me that you liked a girl with a little spit and fire."

***

The door bounced against its frame as Eli marched from the back porch to the barn. He had done his best to control his anger and mumbled under his breath as he fought the urge to look back at the house. No matter how much time had passed or how many nights he lay awake trying to push her face from his mind, the woman still held a spell over his heart. There was something he saw in her that she refused to see herself. From the first day he saw her, he knew there was more to Rebecca Byler than the harsh exterior she showed to everyone else.

***

Smiling slightly, Rebecca waited until his feet exited the porch before moving to the window. There was no doubt about it. She still got under his skin and, for some reason, that pleased her. Was it that she could always count on having the last word, or was it the purple hue his face took on whenever she pushed a little too hard?

She turned from the window and walked to Mary's bedroom through the front room. Gently opening the door, she peered in and was greeted by Mary's soft snores. Pulling the door closed, she turned and rested her hands on her hips and thought. *What now? I don't like chaos, and this house is full of it.*

Stifling her irritation, she picked up an empty cup, straightened a stack of magazines, and headed to the kitchen. How could she tackle the dishes when she clearly told Eli she wasn't his housemaid? *I'm not doing it for him; I'm doing them to help Mary. Maybe she was being unreasonable. There were more important things she could argue about than refusing to wash up a few dishes or sweep the floor. Why did she let him get to her so?*

Opening the refrigerator, she took inventory of what was available to make dinner once Mary woke up. She failed to ask Eli if she had eaten breakfast, but by the look of the plates on the table and the smell of bacon in the air, she assumed she had.

Frustrated and restless, she moved around the kitchen, stacking the dirty dishes next to the basin. She retrieved a tub of hot water from the water reservoir at the back of the wood stove and poured it over a stack of plates in the sink. Once she sunk her hands in the sudsy water, her mind drifted back to a time when she and Eli had high hopes for their future. His certainty and commanding attitude attracted him to her in the first place. Her heart melted into his from the first time he insisted on walking her home. The scene played in her head, and she ached to have a do-over with her life.

Spring five years earlier...

Eli squared his shoulders. "I'm going to walk you home."

"Not may I walk you home,' but 'I'm going to walk you home?' That's a little presumptuous of you, isn't it? What if I don't want you to walk me home?"

Rebecca tucked a piece of hair behind her ear that escaped her kapp and looked down, trying to hide a smirk.

"Look, smarty-pants, I've waited for you to say anything to me that was halfway civil for months now," Eli retorted. "I'm getting tired of waiting. If I'm going to get past your nasty comments, I'm just going to have to take the bull by the horns and get to know you

better. My mommi told me that I couldn't sit around and wait forever for what I wanted. If I want something bad enough, I should go after it."

Removing his hat and wiping the sweat from his brow with the back of his forearm, he said, "Look, I know there are a lot of other girls in our community, but that's not what I want. I like a little spit and fire, and I figure you're just about the only one I know that can keep up with me. So, are you interested or not?"

"That's a pretty unflattering way to tell a girl you're interested in her, don't ya think?"

"Maybe, but as I said, I'm tired of beating around the bush and playing it safe. I decided to go all in. Are you in or not?"

"Can I at least think about it for a minute?"

"I'll give you one minute. Sixty, fifty-nine, fifty-eight, fifty-seven, fifty-six ..."

"Stop! I'll let you walk me home, but that's all I'm promising right now."

"All right, I guess that's a start. But I'm tired of waiting and I'm not going to give you long to make up your mind."

Catching up to his long strides, Rebecca fell in step beside him. Anna and Emma were snickering as she passed, and she put a quick finger to her lips, pleading with them to keep quiet.

"Why did you have to pick the most public place around to go after what you want? We'll be the topic of conversation tomorrow at church."

"I figured I'd put my claim on you since I wasn't getting anywhere talking to you all gentleman-like. Every time I tried to strike up a conversation, you looked like you'd rather bite my head off. A guy wants a girl to give him a friendly smile once in a while, and the way I see it, smiles aren't in your repertoire, and I'm about to change that."

"What makes you think I want you to change it?"

"And you don't?"

She stopped dead in her tracks, waiting for him to notice she wasn't walking beside him. She gave up when he didn't slow down and ran to catch up to him.

"You didn't answer me."

With a huff, she asked, "I'm not sure what I'm supposed to be answering; you've thrown so many things at me."

"To start with, why don't you smile? What makes you look so sour all the time?"

Rebecca felt her nose start to tingle and a lump form in her throat. Taking in a deep breath, she willed herself not to cry in front of him. She wouldn't give him the satisfaction of letting him know he had upset her.

"You are the rudest boy I know."

"I suppose so, but I've tried to be nice and look where it got me. Months of trying to get your attention and nothing. Today was the first day that you've given me even a hint of a smile, and I took it as my only chance."

Stopping in the middle of the road, Eli grabbed her arm and made her stop and turn toward him. As she jerked his hand off her arm, he noticed she had big tears spilling down her cheeks. His stomach flipped, and he wasn't sure if it was from the spark that ignited when he touched her or the fact that he had made her cry.

"I'm only going to say one more thing, and then I'll let you be," he said as he tugged on the same piece of hair that she had tucked behind her ear earlier. "A girl as pretty as you should wear more smiles."

He turned and walked away, leaving her at the end of her parent's driveway. There were so many things she wanted to say, but the lump in her throat had prevented her from saying a word. She was mad that he held nothing back and told her just what he thought of her. She was sad that he saw her as a sourpuss because that wasn't how she wanted the world to see her, especially him. It was his grandmother that made her realize that a smile could make a difference. But most of all, she wanted him to know that she was interested, and that she'd love to learn to keep up with both his snide remarks and his long strides.

Rebecca wiped her eyes with her sleeve, remembering the warmth she felt when Eli grabbed her arm. He thinks I'm pretty. She felt a smile replace her tears. He's right! I should wear more smiles.

She stood and watched him walk away until she could only see the top of his straw hat over the crest of the hill. Feeling hopeful and determined, she turned and walked down her parents' driveway, thinking of everything she'd say to him if she got a chance. And maybe if she gave him one of her prettiest smiles, he'd offer to take her home from the singeon tomorrow night.

But now, standing in his grandmother's kitchen, she knew a do-over wasn't in the cards. She had said too much, betrayed his loyalty, and let him believe she was in love with another. All to protect him from the inevitable doom that was sure to follow her throughout the rest of her life.

History was repeating itself. She was sure of it. The undisclosed secret sin she harbored was pushing its way through her soul just like the dandelions that invaded Mary's garden.

Thinking back on how much peace her father found when he finally told Emma of her biological family, she wondered if she could see the same peace. Perhaps if she confessed the sin that put a wedge between Eli and herself, she could find relief.

But she was sure her secret would be too much for even Eli's forgiving heart to accept. It was too much for her to bear; how could she expect anyone else to understand what her selfishness had caused? No, she couldn't do it. It was better to keep pushing everyone she loved away in hopes of protecting them from the dreadfulness that followed her.

Drying her hands on a towel, she heard Mary's small voice carry through the house. "Eli, are you there?"

Rebecca pushed open the bedroom door and moved to Mary's side.

"Oh, Rebecca, you came."

She replied, placing her hand under Mary's elbow, and helping her stand. "I did, even though I'm not sure why you requested me and not Anna. She is much more suited to care for you."

Mary's eyes narrowed as she winced in pain. "But it's not Anna I want taking care of me; it's you."

Moving Mary's cane closer to her grip, Rebecca asked, "For heaven's sake. Why?"

"All in good time, my child. For now, get this old woman to the bathroom. I'm in dire need of a bath, and that's your task for the day."

Rebecca guided Mary to the bathroom, still trying to make sense of the woman's chatter about choosing her over Anna. Hoping she could gain more insight into her comment, she inquired, "I still don't understand why you would want me and not Anna."

Mary stopped moving and looked up at her. "Not now." There was an edge to her voice. "I need a bath."

Rebecca had never seen this side of Mary. Sharp, to the point, and impatient. Mary was full of life and a true joy to be around in the past. It was she who gave her reason to smile all those years ago.

As she readied Mary for a long soak in the tub, she drifted off to a time so many years ago when Mary explained her outlook on life.

Five years earlier…

Rebecca pulled a chair closer to Mary and asked, "How do you stay so happy? You always have a smile on your face."

The older woman just smiled. Pausing for a few minutes, she finally answered, "I guess I believe if you can't have the best of everything, you make the best of everything you have. As I see it, God wants us to see the good around us, and there is no sense in being unhappy; it's not going to change anything other than make us blue. And I don't like to feel that way."

Mary stopped talking long enough to pop a juicy strawberry in her mouth and turned toward Rebecca.

"I feel blessed, and to me, that's enough to keep a smile on my face," Mary continued, "I may not have a lot of money, but I figure a smile is free, and I give them away whenever I can. You never know when someone you meet might be having a rough day. A friendly smile could be just what they need."

The frail woman in front of her was but a mere image of the woman she first met five years ago. Gone was the welcoming smile and bubbly personality she had come to love. After filling the bathtub, she helped Mary undress, and all but lifted her into the warm water. Her petite frame was easy to maneuver, and she dutifully washed her hair and transparent skin. It was all Rebecca could do to pray that she would once again witness the part of Mary that her stroke shamelessly took away.

CHAPTER 4

E li's mother voice cracked, "I knew this would happen. If you had only listened to us, you wouldn't find yourself in this predicament now."

Eli sighed. "But *Mamm*, if I had listened to you, *Mommi* wouldn't have anyone here taking care of her."

"Eli, your father and I only wanted the best for you. It was your choice to leave Lancaster to tend to your grandfather's failing sheep farm. You made your bed; now you must lie in it."

His mother's voice took on a familiar edge. "When are you going to come to your senses and come home? It's high time you start living your own life and stop living for her. I'd say it's about time you find yourself a wife."

Eli rubbed his forehead and switched the receiver to his other hand. He knew there was an underlying bitterness between his grandmother and his parents that he never entirely understood. It was exhausting trying to keep peace on the never-ending teeter-totter of grudges and secrets he wasn't privy to. Would it ever end? Why couldn't they both understand God instructs them to forgive and forget and move on? *Mommi* Mary didn't have much time left on this earth, and they all needed to get past this.

"Look, *Mamm,* all I'm asking is for you to get *Datt* to come visit her. She keeps asking for him, and I could use some help around here for a few weeks."

"I doubt your *datt* will be up for that. He has his hands full on this farm, and besides, it's planting season. He'll want to be here supervising your *bruders*. How about we send you some money?"

"I don't need money. What I need is for the both of you to act like you care."

Maybe calling his parents wasn't such a good idea. What made him think his *datt* would care about anyone but himself? He proved that more than once over the last few years.

"I'll give your *datt* your message, but I wouldn't count on him breaking free from the farm to come to Willow Springs anytime soon."

"*Mamm,* God called me here."

When she didn't say anything, he knew he had surprised her. Did her silence denote her displeasure in his comment?

"Son, I know you felt called to take care of your grandmother, but what you don't understand goes so far back in history; I don't even understand it myself."

"What is it that tore *Datt* away from Willow Springs? Why is there so much animosity toward *Mommi?* She has such a kind heart. What on earth could have ever happened that he can't even stomach coming to visit her?"

"I'm not really sure. But perhaps your grandmother holds the key. I learned long ago not to press your *datt* on the subject."

He was quiet for a moment. "It makes no sense."

"I agree, son. But often, when things like this fester for so long, it's best to leave them buried in the past and move on."

"That's just it. If whatever it is that's keeping *Datt* from spending time with his mother stays buried, the woman will have no peace. Please, *Mamm,* try to convince him to come see her."

"I'll do what I can, but I won't make any promises."

"That's all I can ask for. One more thing."

"What's that?"

"What do you know about *Mommi's* family from Lancaster?"

"Not much. Only bits and pieces. She didn't have any siblings since her mother died in childbirth. Her father left to serve in a field hospital in France during World War II. Before he left, he sent Mary to live with his neighbor, your Great-Grandfather Bricker. Shortly after her father returned, Mary and your grandfather married and moved to Willow Springs. As far as I know, she doesn't have any family left here in Lancaster."

"Why did they move so far from home? The Bricker Farm was huge even back then. There would have been plenty of work for him."

She gave a dry laugh. "Eli, you know as well as I do it's not best to dig things up from the past. No good will come from it."

Eli sighed heavily. "Okay, I'll leave it alone. But there is something that just doesn't sit just right. I think if I could get to the bottom of it…"

"You've spent too much time with your grandmother. Her white-picket-fence syndrome she has just isn't going to happen, so leave it in the past."

After they said their goodbyes, Eli sat in the phone shanty and thought. *What could have happened to cause so much animosity on his father's part? His mother made it sound like she knew more than she let on. Could the estrangement between his grandmother and his father be more than a minor family squabble? Or was there something far deeper that could be resolved if it was only addressed?*

***

After a warm bath and a hot cup of tea, Mary sat near the window. From across the yard, she watched as Eli shut the door of the phone shanty and headed back toward the barn. His slumped shoulders reminded her of the heavy burden he carried. If it was the last thing she'd do, she would find a way to bring Rebecca and him back together. He needed a wife to share his heavy load. There had to be more to their short romance since either of them failed to find someone else to share their life with.

Rebecca's footsteps stopped short of her chair. "I was going to start some dinner. Anything you have a liking for?"

It didn't take but a second for her response. "Chicken and dumplings."

"But that will take hours."

"If you didn't want me to give you my desire, why ask?"

"True. I'll think twice next time."

Mary smiled as Rebecca walked away and tapped her quad stick on the floor to get her attention. "Remember, I'm paying you, so I'd put a smile on your face and get to it."

It didn't take but a few minutes for the clang of pots and pans to make an awful racket from the other room. With each sound, Mary smiled broader, she had tricked Rebecca into making Eli's favorite meal. One thing for sure was the best way to a man's heart was through his stomach, and she was sure it was the same for her grandson as well.

***

Rebecca mumbled under her breath as she unwrapped the chicken and added onion, celery, carrots, and a bay leaf to a pot. Rummaging through cupboards, looking for the correct array of spices, she added the mix to the pan and filled it with water.

Adding a few pieces of kindling to the wood stove, she moved the pan to the burner and finished putting away the dishes she'd washed earlier. Without realizing it, she caught herself peering out the kitchen window, hoping to catch a glimpse of Eli. Disgusted with herself for even caring where he was, she moved away from the window and picked up Mary's recipe box, fingering through the well-worn cards. Stopping on the second chocolate-stained card, it read *Eli's Favorite Brownies.*

A good dose of chocolate was precisely what the day called for, regardless of if it was Eli's favorite or not.

Just before noon, the house was filled with the rich aroma of a family dinner, and she looked forward to Mary and Eli joining her in the kitchen. Eli could be heard on the back porch stomping the mud off his boots.

With her back toward the door, she held her breath and waited for him to say something before she turned around.

***

Eli watched the clock in the barn and wondered if Rebecca had made enough dinner for both him and Mary. The mere thought of the girl he prayed so fervently for taking up residence in his kitchen left him bewildered. He really didn't want to go down that path again with Rebecca, but at this point, he would do anything his grandmother wanted to ensure she was well cared for.

Eli kicked the mud off his boots before opening the kitchen door. Shocked at the kitchen's transformation in such a short time, he stated, "I do believe you clearly said you wouldn't be cleaning up after me or making me any meals."

She swung around and dried her hands on a towel. "I didn't. I made Mary dinner, and if I wanted to do so, I had to wash the dishes first."

He moved to the stove and picked up the lid from the simmering pot. "Chicken and dumplings?"

"That's pretty obvious, isn't it?"

Eli snapped his head in her direction in hopes of a smile to soften her sharp words. Instead, he was met with a sneer that would chase any logical man for the hills.

He replaced the lid and moved to the sink. The cool water flowing over his hands did little to settle the hairs on the back of his neck. For his grandmother's sake, he needed to find a way to make this new arrangement work. With Rebecca's feral cat-like tendencies, it was going to be a challenge, to say the least.

Before he could comment on her snide remarks, Mary's long slow shuffle made its way to the table. He scurried to pull her chair out and placed his hand under her good elbow to help her ease down. Her limp arm hung at her waist, and she pulled it to her lap.

Eli pushed her chair in closer to the table and moved her quad stick to the side of the counter before taking a seat.

He patted the back of her hand. "So, how is my favorite *Mommi* today?"

In a slightly slurred mumble, Mary replied, "First, I'm anything but good with being so incapable of tending to myself. However, Rebecca helped me with a bath, and I feel like a new woman. Or as much as I can with this broken body."

"Well, she definitely earned her keep if she's made you feel like a new woman again."

He raised his eyebrow in Rebecca's direction, and she made a loud TSK sound as she placed a steaming bowl in front of him.

After they bowed their heads and Eli tapped his spoon on the side of his bowl, indicating he was through, Rebecca tucked a napkin on Mary's lap. The small gesture touched Eli, but he refused to acknowledge it for fear she'd lash out in front of his grandmother.

Turning his attention to Mary, he said, "I called my *mamm* this morning and invited them to come for a visit as you requested. She wasn't too hopeful that they could pull themselves away from the farm during planting season."

Mary stirred her spoon around the bowl and struggled to take a bite without spilling it down her dress. Both Eli and Rebecca watched and were ready to offer assistance if need be. When she let her spoon sink to the side of the dish, she whispered, "I really didn't think they could, but I appreciate you asking. I know how busy they are these days."

Eli took a drink. "I'm sorry, but *Datt* shouldn't be too busy to visit with his mother. I'll never understand him."

Mary picked up her napkin. "Andy bowed out of my life long before any of this happened."

"But it's just not right."

"Maybe so, but it's just how it is," Mary said the words, but down deep inside, she was crying at the loss of her son. If he only knew the sacrifices his father made on his behalf, things might have been different. But was it her place to go back on the promises she made to her husband and take their secret to the grave? It seemed like the right thing to do when she made that vow. *But don't Andy and Eli deserve to know the truth?* She

66

couldn't help but think. *Oh, Andy, how could you do this to me after everything your father gave up for you? We loved you and were there for you every step of the way, and this is the thanks I get. Total abandonment. You pushed my care onto your own son when it should be you taking care of me. Eli has a life of his own to live. He should be settling down with a family, not caring for an ailing grandmother.*

"*Mommi*?" Her grandson's voice pulled her back to the present. Nothing he could say would cure the deeply etched pain she anguished over. Only God could take her pain away, and she wished for that more and more with each passing day.

"*Mommi*, what is it?"

"Nothing a nice long nap won't cure. You finish eating. Rebecca, if you'll help me to my room, I think I should lay down for a spell."

Eli laid his spoon down and started to get up, but Rebecca stopped him. "I got this. Do as your grandmother said and finish eating." He gave in to both strong-willed women. He waited until Rebecca led her away from the table before finishing his meal.

The underlying pain followed the creases on his grandmother's face so deep that he instantly became annoyed with his father all over again. Why couldn't he see that it was his mother's last wish to see him, perhaps for the last time? He carried his bowl to the sink, cut a brownie from the pan near the stove, and headed back to the barn.

Once outside, he gathered his bucket of fencing supplies and headed out to walk the fence line. He thought over everything he knew about his Great-Grandfather Bricker and what he'd heard about his own father going to live with him right before he died. Why did he leave the farm to his father and not one of his own sons?

Nothing made much sense, and what did wasn't good. There was an underlying hostility between his father and his grandparents throughout his whole life. He had the feeling he should go see his father, no matter the cost. And that cost would be high. He could count on that. His father was pretty set in his ways, and he didn't like anyone to challenge him, especially his own son.

Still, seeds of unrest were taking root and growing inside of him that wouldn't be put to rest until he figured out what happened to make his father turn on his own mother like he had. But he couldn't do that during lambing season. It would have to wait until summer at the earliest. He prayed his *mommi* would stay strong until then.

***

Rebecca helped Mary sit on the edge of the bed and removed her black sneakers before she lifted her legs to the mattress. "Is there anything I can bring you?"

"No, dear, I think a nap is all I need. Thank you for making dinner. I'm sure Eli enjoyed it."

"I don't really care if Eli did. I made it for you, and you didn't even eat anything."

Mary laid her head back on her pillow. "You do care, and you're not fooling this old woman for one minute."

Rebecca pulled a blanket up over her and shook her head. "I have no idea what you're talking about. Whatever notions you have about Eli and me, they can fly right out the window. I'm here for you only, and if I could have figured out a way to get out of that, I would have."

"Whatever you say, my dear. But remember, God's plans are not always our own."

"Mary, you're talking nonsense, and you're living in the past. Whatever you thought would happen five years ago is all dead and gone. Too much time has passed, and too much water has flowed under that bridge."

When she stood to leave, Mary's eyes were already fluttering closed, and she waved her off with her good hand. After all these years, why do Mary's comments affect her so, and why does the pain of giving everything up to protect Eli matter now? It was nobody's fault but her own, and no amount of wishful thinking from a dying woman should make a hill of beans now.

She pulled Mary's bedroom door closed softly and stood at the front window watching a cluster of robins peck at the thawing ground. She couldn't help but think her life was much like those birds poking and prodding for just one juicy worm. Hopping from one hole to the next, hoping it would be the one to fill her up.

Over the last five years, she'd pushed everyone away, put on a rugged exterior that no one could break through, and was determined to keep the sins of her past hidden so deep they wouldn't show their ugly head to anyone she held dear.

But that was just it. Everyone she loved didn't love her. And whose fault was that? Hers, of course. It was better that way. Or so she thought.

She moved the chicken pot to the warming spot on the stove and walked to the counter. Eli had tipped the sugar dish on its side and wrote *THANK YOU!* in the fine white crystals.

A gentle nudging softened her heart for a split second before it became a push, and she focused on the exclamation point. Was that his way of being sarcastic? She brushed the sugar back in the bowl and tried to figure out what was bothering her so.

Not that God ever answered her prayers in the past, but she felt drawn to lift her questions to Him.

Why now? That part of my heart has been closed tight for years. Is this your way of punishing me? Haven't I sacrificed enough? What more do you want from me?

CHAPTER 5

Emma poured Samuel a cup of coffee and stirred in the right amount of sugar and cream to add a smile to his face before handing it to him.

She sat down beside him at the table and brushed a few loose toast crumbs off the table in her hand. "I'm not so sure Rebecca will be open to the idea of spending any more time with me than she absolutely has to.

"I'm not high on her list of casual acquaintances these days."

"Now Emma, she's your *schwester,* and if we can't offer our own kin grace, how can we expect God to offer it to us?"

"But she can't stand the sight of me. Everything that comes out of my mouth infuriates her, and I'm not sure why."

"Like I said before, her secrets built a wall around her heart, keeping her from finding peace. I'm sure of it."

"You keep saying that, but what are those secrets? Maybe if I knew, I could help her work her way through them."

"They're not mine to tell. The only one I can reveal is the one that affected me personally."

Emma emptied the crumbs onto a napkin and anxiously waited for Samuel's explanation.

Samuel reached out and took her hands in his. "Now, before I tell you about my part in all this, please know I'm as much to blame as Rebecca. I don't want you to hold any ill feelings toward your *schwester*. It was my fault for letting it go on for as long as it did. I have made my peace with God, but I know I need to make my peace with Eli as well."

"Eli, why Eli?"

"Hold on, give me a minute to explain."

"You're worrying me. What could have happened that was so bad you had to make it right with God?"

Samuel squeezed her fingertips. "Believe me, I've carried around enough guilt about that summer for a lifetime. But God showed me there is no room in my life for Him and guilt."

Emma moved in closer. "Please, Samuel, tell me. What is it?"

"Okay, here goes. Remember the summer you went to Sugarcreek to get to know your birth mother?"

"*Jah.*"

"Well, that was also the summer Rebecca and Eli were seen leaving the *singeons* together. It was no news to anyone that Eli had his eyes set on her. But then something happened, and suddenly, Rebecca begged me to help her end it."

"But why would she need your help? Since when does a girl need help to end a courtship?"

Samuel averted his eyes from Emma's and whispered, "I had witnessed something and kept it to myself. I became just as guilty by not acknowledging my part in it, and she held it over me. I felt I had no choice but to do her bidding."

Emma pulled her hands from his grip. "You let my *schwester* blackmail you?"

"There's so much more to all this, but again, it's not my story to tell. It's hers, and until Rebecca does, she will always be stuck in this vicious cycle of hurt and anger."

"But what did you do, and why do you need to make peace with Eli?"

"That's just it. What I took part in affected Eli in a big way."

"Please, Samuel, just spit it out. What did you do?"

Samuel leaned back and grabbed the arms of the polished oak chair. "I made Eli believe I was in love with her."

"You what? Why on earth would you do that?"

"Rebecca didn't want him to think there was any chance for them. I helped her make him believe we were courting."

Emma rubbed her fingers over both temples. "So let me get this straight. My *schwester*, who knew how I felt about you, went behind my back and forced you into deceiving someone who cared for her. What kind of *schwester* does that?"

Samuel reached out and picked up her hand again. "The kind of girl who is lost in her own pain."

"But she's been mad at me for what reason? She has been acting like I'm the one who's done something wrong all these years. With all due respect, she's the one who's been harboring an unresolved secret. It put a wedge between us. She's blamed it on me when it's been her own doing all along."

"Emma, calm down. I've given it a lot of thought and prayer over the years. I believe secrets can cause a great deal of harm to a person, which is what I think has happened with Rebecca."

Emma took in a labored breath and blew it out before responding. "We think secrets can lay dormant in our mind, forever buried deep in the past, but at some point, they come alive and have a will of their own. They destroy our lives, and until we turn them over to God and fully find redemption, they will eat away at us until we have no choice but to surrender them to Jesus."

She leaned her elbows on the table. "I don't understand. If it's just one secret, why wouldn't she want to confess and be done with it?"

"That's just it. My involvement in helping her convince Eli there was no hope for them was just one little aspect of a much larger problem. Until she finds it in her heart to confess the whole truth to the Lord and all those involved, she won't get much relief from her past."

"But what can I do? Rebecca has her own agenda. Spending time with me is at the bottom of her list. She never has time for anyone but herself."

"Exactly why we are on the mission we're on. If we haven't learned anything else in the past six months, it's that God will continue to lead our way if we are open to following Him. I believe we're meant to be the light in Rebecca's darkness. And I know for a fact I already failed miserably at that."

"How so?"

"To begin with, I laid into her the other day about how she treated you at the bakery. All that did was ruffle her feathers even more. But more importantly, it made me hear God even clearer. It's not our job to change her heart; it's God's. All we can do is help her grow in Christ."

"But Samuel, do you know what that means?"

"I do. It means there may come a time when we can show her that her past doesn't define her future, and if she turns her life over to Jesus, she can find the peace she is longing for."

Emma stood and carried their cups to the sink. "But it also means we open up our private bible studies to her, and that may open up a whole new can of worms."

Samuel walked to the sink, wrapped his arms around her waist, rested his chin on top of her starched white *kapp,* and whispered, "I am the vine; you are the branches..."

Emma laid her hands on his chest and pushed him back enough so she could look into his eyes. "I understand we are to be God's branches, but how can we do anything to help her if she's not willing to confess whatever is haunting her?"

"That's just it. Secrets want out. They have a way of trying to escape."

Emma pulled away from his hold and picked up more of the breakfast dishes from the table. "By keeping it hidden, she's pushed everyone away in the process. All she has ever wanted is to be accepted, but that can't happen as long as there are parts of her that she's keeping under lock and key. That's why there's never been any hope for her and Eli. As long as she keeps things from him, there will never be any hope for a future."

Samuel leaned back on the counter and crossed his arms over his chest. "Exactly. The very act of secrecy makes us inaccessible to love."

"Oh, Samuel, it's like history is repeating itself. Remember when my *datt* kept my true identity a secret for so long? When the time came and he needed to tell me, he became impossible to live with. He pushed me away and became angry. It's the same thing Rebecca is doing. Why can't she see it?"

"Because she's too deep in it to realize what's happening."

Emma ran hot water over the stack of dishes and tossed Samuel a towel. "But what can we do?"

"Pray and remember what Alvin and Lynette taught us. Without faith, a person can't understand spiritual problems."

Emma handed him a wet plate. "And we can't counsel an unbeliever. All we can do is evangelize to them. And that's exactly what we can do for Rebecca. She might not enjoy it, but I'll pray God gives us the wisdom to make a difference in her life."

***

In the distance, Rebecca heard a rooster announcing the first rays of light above the horizon. Caught somewhere between a dream and reality, she heard laughter. Fighting to remain in the peace of slumber, she let her mind follow the sound.

Walking through a field of clover, she stopped short of the row of maple trees that lined Willow Creek and watched three young girls playing by the bank. As if she was watching the scene for the first time, she stood back and remembered the day as if it were yesterday.

"Come on, Rebecca, Mamm won't mind if we're a few minutes late for dinner. As long as we stay near the bank and don't go in too deep, we'll be fine."

"But we were supposed to go to Shetler's Grocery and come right home. If we're late, she'll be worried, and I'll be the one who gets in trouble."

Rebecca watched the younger version of herself walk to the creek's edge. "Emma, Anna, come on, we have to go."

"But Rebecca, it's hot. Please…just for a few minutes? We'll wrap our skirts up high, so they don't get wet. Mamm will never know."

The young girl looked over her shoulder toward the field where their datt was plowing. "All right, but just for a few minutes. Mamm will come looking for us if we don't get back soon. If she finds out I let you go in the creek after yesterday's heavy rain, she'll have my tail."

In a flash, the day turned dark, and the murky waters of Willow Creek swam through her lungs as she thrashed her arms, trying to find her footing on the muddy banks. Under the water, her schwester's screams bounced off the ripples. In an instant, a log appeared, and she wrapped her arm around the floating limb and pulled herself to the surface. Floating in the fast current, she let the log pull her downstream, all while watching Emma and Anna run along the bank, hollering in her direction.

Anna took off toward the field, and Emma's little feet tried hard to keep up with her in the water. "Hold tight, Rebecca. Please ... Rebecca, hold on. Anna went to get Datt!

The sound of Emma's voice faded even though Rebecca fought to remain in the past. When the rooster's call became louder than the cries of her youngest *schwester,* the reality of what she lost became all too real. Rebecca pulled her quilt up over her head and sunk down deep under the covers. Once she threw back the covers and faced the day, she knew that the memory of what she used to have would be lost again forever.

She ignored the knock on her bedroom door for as long as she could. Anna pushed open the door and walked to the edge of her bed, shaking her from her dream-like state.

"Rebecca, you better get up. *Datt* and Wilma are waiting for breakfast, and you need to get to Mary's. Best not be late on your second day."

Anna pulled the blanket from her head, and she retaliated. "Stop! I'll get up when I'm good and ready, and I'm not there yet."

Anna threw her arms up. "Suit yourself. Just figured you'd rather get a visit from me than Wilma. She's already in a mood because the eggs are getting cold."

Rebecca tossed the blanket to the bottom of the bed and sat up. "All right already. I'm up. Now get out of here, so I can get dressed. I'll be down in a minute."

The first rays of the sun were starting to shine their way into her room; a heaviness surrounded her thoughts. *Love like that doesn't last forever, I'm sure of it. Emma wouldn't care at all about me drowning these days.*

She walked into the kitchen without saying a word, lured by the aroma of fresh coffee and salted ham. Taking her seat and bowing her head, she ignored the irritated glare from her stepmother. She waited until her father cleared his throat before opening her eyes.

Anna reached for a slice of toast and asked, "How was Mary yesterday?"

Rebecca added a scoop of eggs to her plate. "There aren't a lot of things she can do by herself, let alone take care of that house. I'm not sure why she is so set on staying put in Willow Springs when her son lives in Lancaster. Surely he's better equipped to take care of her than Eli is."

Wilma passed the plate of ham and added, "Hence why they need a nursemaid. I surely hope you're treating them both kindly."

Rebecca's heart pounded; anger poured through her before she responded, "Who do you think I am?"

The table fell quiet, and a wave of remorse brushed by her like an annoying fly. Had she overreacted to Wilma's comment, or was it the shame she felt by her harsh treatment of Eli yesterday? If her father found out how she spoke to him, he'd have more than a few choice words to say.

Jacob pounded his fork on the table. "You apologize to Wilma. There was no need to speak to her in that tone."

"She automatically thinks the worst of me."

Her father picked up his knife and cut his ham. "And have you given her reason to believe otherwise?"

"That doesn't matter. What matters is she's always free to offer her opinion even when it's not asked for!"

Wilma laid her hand on Jacob's forearm. "It's fine. Rebecca's old enough to know that if she lets one bad weed grow in her garden, it will choke all the good from growing and taking root."

Rebecca rolled her eyes and pushed her plate away. "What's that supposed to mean?"

Anna took a sip of her tea before saying, "She's trying to say it's your responsibility to plant your garden with seeds of kindness."

Without saying a word, Rebecca carried her plate to the sink and headed out the back door. The early morning breeze made her wish she would have grabbed a sweater, but instead of going back inside, she picked up her pace. The short walk to Eli and Mary's did little to calm her frustration at Anna taking Wilma's side. The one person she could always count on having her back just turned on her as well.

As she walked past Emma and Samuel's, their chocolate lab, Someday, ran out to greet her. She stopped, knelt down, hugged his furry coat, and let him nuzzle her neck.

"How's my big guy today?"

Someday used his nose to force her hand into a back scratch, and she giggled as he leaned into her fingertips. "That feels good, doesn't it, big guy?"

Emma walked up beside her. "He sure does love his back scratched. I've never seen a dog who can force a stranger into a good back rub."

Rebecca stood back up and sneered. "I'm anything but a stranger."

Emma patted the top of the dog's head. "I didn't mean you were a stranger. I just meant that he could encourage anyone to love on him a bit."

Emma sucked in a calming breath, trying to remember everything Samuel and she had just spoken about. "I'm glad I caught you this morning. I was hoping you might like to come to supper sometime this week. It's been a long time since we've spent any time together, and I'd hoped we might find a way to clear the air between us."

"Why would you think I'd want to do that?"

"I don't know. Maybe because I miss you, and I'd love to figure out what's eating at you."

Both women stood in the middle of the road waiting for the other to speak first. When the silence became uncomfortable, Emma turned and walked away saying, "The invitation stands. You are welcome at my table anytime."

Rebecca watched as Emma returned to the basket waiting for her at the clothesline. After she was sure she wasn't going to turn back around, she headed back down the road toward Eli's.

After the horrible way she had treated her earlier in the week, she was astonished that her little *schwester* still wanted

86

anything to do with her. If the roles were reversed, she was confident that inviting her to share a meal would be the last thing on her mind.

Not one prone to cry, Rebecca blinked back tears and looked down at the road. She wished things could be different. She wished she could tell Emma how she had betrayed her trust and forced Samuel to lie for her.

Some things were better off left buried deep in the past. Much like the one lie that would haunt her the rest of her life. Even if she wanted to confess, too much time had passed. God had already punished Emma and Samuel by taking their child before he even had a chance to live. It was all her fault.

It was too late. Her fate was sealed. She would continue to push everyone away, so when it came time for God to punish her, no one would miss her, and life could go on without her.

CHAPTER 6

The aftermath of Emma's invitation still burned on Rebecca's cheeks as she walked up Eli's driveway. Along both sides of the loose gravel path were fenced-in pastures with abundant herds of sheep. Eli had turned every ounce of his grandfather's farm into pasture except the acre-sized yard. A weed-filled kitchen and flower garden and an array of flowerpots dotted the landscape surrounding the white clapboard one-story farmhouse.

Walking down the path that led to the kitchen door, she stopped to pinch a stem of mint pushing its way through a patch of weeds and gathered a cluster of Johnny Jump-ups. She pulled the mint to her nose, and it reminded her of the Sweet Meadow Tea her *mamm* used to make.

Still lost in a time long gone, she didn't hear Eli step up beside her and leaped at his voice.

Eli grinned. "Didn't mean to startle you."

Rebecca rolled her eyes. "Oh, no, you didn't."

Both stood looking out over the weed patch that was once a reflection of Mary's love for plants.

Eli sighed. "Not much time left in the day after I tend to two hundred sheep to take care of such things."

Rebecca didn't look up at Eli. "I suppose if I have time, I could at least get some of the weeds pulled." Before she even got the words out of her mouth, she regretted doing so. What did she know about gardening? To be honest, half the time, she couldn't tell a weed from a plant. That was always Emma's job growing up. She preferred to be in the barn tending to her alpacas than working in the gardens.

Rebecca looked up, stricken, hoping he wouldn't take her up on the offer.

Eli pointed to the bench alongside the garden. "I bet *Mommi* Mary would love to sit outside with you when it warms up."

He walked past her and around to the back of the house. Leaving her standing in the same spot where she wished she could turn back the minutes. *What have I done now? Always opening my mouth before I think. I have no desire to play in the dirt, that's for sure and certain.*

***

Eli grinned from ear to ear as he left Rebecca standing, trying to take her words back. He remembered a lot about Rebecca Byler, including her dislike of gardening. But if anyone could teach someone about tending a garden, it would be his grandmother. And besides, a little sunshine would do them both some good.

When he pushed the wheelbarrow filled with a rake, shovel, and pruning shears around the house, her mouth fell open, but no words escaped. "I think you should have everything you might need. Let me know if you don't, and I'll get on it."

"Now hold on just a minute. When you hired me, you didn't say anything about cleaning up an overgrown garden. I doubt that's in my job duties. I take back my offer. I wasn't thinking."

He gave her a halfhearted grin as he brushed by her but refused to answer. Her tone spoke a thousand words, and he knew better than to engage in a sparring match with her. In the

back of his mind, he kept hearing his grandmother tell him …
just cultivate a friendship with her…

He wasn't sure what that meant other than he knew the heart
of Rebecca Byler held more than the brassy exterior she showed
to everyone else. He'd been given a second chance to be around
the green-eyed beauty that captured his heart so many years
ago. And in the dark of the night, he proclaimed before God that
he wasn't about to let the few daggers she kept throwing at him
wear him down. If He gave him another chance to fix what was
broken with his Becca, he'd do as God bid.

He didn't dare turn around as he walked back to the barn.
He could feel her eyes burning a hole through his shirt as clearly
as if she held a knife in her hand. Thinking to himself, *She
offered; I only took her up on the idea before she had a chance
to change her mind.*

No sooner did he make his way through the opened double
doors than he heard his neighbor, Samuel Yoder, call his name.

"Hello, Eli. Are you in here?"

"*Jah*, back here."

Eli lifted his head above the gate where he was stooped
down, checking on a pregnant ewe. He opened and closed the

gate and latched it tight before extending his hand in Samuel's direction. "What do I owe this visit to?"

Samuel drew in a long breath and replied, "This visit is way overdue. I'm hoping you have a few minutes so we could discuss a matter I should've cleared up years ago."

Eli had no idea what Samuel was referring to. By the way Samuel's forehead was crunched together; he assumed it was serious.

***

Heart still thumping, Rebecca pushed open the back door, laid the handful of miniature pansies on the counter, and slipped out of her mud-caked black shoes. Mary sat in a chair pulled up close to the window that overlooked the backyard. In not much more than a whisper, she said, "It really was quite glorious in the spring."

Rebecca walked beside her. "What's that?"

"When in bloom, the pink rhododendrons cover the fence so much that you can't see the fence through the flowers. They don't bloom until June, though."

Rebecca stooped down so she could see what Mary was pointing to. All they both could see were barren branches with just a hint of green buds starting to change the landscape. Mary knew she didn't know the difference, but she acted as she did for her sake.

Mary couldn't speak past the lump in her throat as she watched Rebecca add the small bouquet of pansies to a tiny juice glass and set it on the windowsill. Mary's throat closed tight, and she gasped for air.

Rebecca snapped around at the sound and ran to her side. "What is it?" The room fell silent, and tears streamed down Mary's cheeks.

Rebecca looked deep into Mary's eyes but couldn't read her expression. Was she in pain? For the first time in a long time, Rebecca felt something that resembled compassion, and her heart sank.

The old woman's eyes misted over and focused on the small vase on the windowsill. "Where did you find those?"

"They were at the edge of the garden right beside a patch of mint."

Through a labored hiccup, she asked, "Bring them to me."

Rebecca carried the tiny glass container to her side and handed it off to her. When she thought Mary had a good grip on the glass, she let go, and it slipped from her frail fingers and shattered on the floor. Mary dropped her head, and her shoulders sank, pulling her petite frame into a childlike form.

Rebecca's eyes flickered, and she tried to keep her irritation at the unexpected mess under control. When she bent down to pick up the shattered glass, she felt Mary's eyes looking down at her. Rebecca felt her pain long before she saw the darkness in her eyes. Did she dare pry?

Before she had a chance to say a word, Mary pointed to the bathroom, and they went on about their day. Rebecca took care of Mary's needs for the rest of the morning, tidied up the house, and made dinner. For the first time, someone other than herself occupied her mind. Something in Mary's eyes spoke of a deep-etched sadness that bothered Rebecca. It was as if they shared the same cell in a darkened room for a split second. What was it, and how could she explain it?

When Eli didn't come in for the noon-time meal, she wandered from window to window throughout the house, hoping to catch sight of him. An edge of bitterness and resentment welled up inside her because she went out of her way to make enough for him, and he didn't come in to eat. A spark of anger lit inside her just as the screen door slammed.

She had her back to the kitchen, sitting on the living room floor sorting through years' worth of seed catalogs as Eli rummaged through the kitchen. He didn't say a word and moved throughout the room without acknowledging her. Something was wrong; she could feel it. There was a tension in the air that was much different from their early morning interaction.

Stacking the most recent issues on the stand next to Mary's chair, she picked up a large stack of old magazines and carried them to the trash in the kitchen.

In a gruff voice, Eli said, "Just leave them by the door. I'll take care of them."

Dropping the stack on the floor by the back door, Rebecca placed both hands on her hips and replied, "Is it something I said?"

Eli buttered two slices of bread, forked a slice of meatloaf up off the plate, and made a sandwich before pushing the plate aside.

Rebecca clicked her tongue when he laid the butter-filled knife on the clean table and wiped up the mess before saying,

"If you had come in at noon, you wouldn't have to eat cold meatloaf."

After taking a bite, Eli rubbed his temple with his free hand.

"Do you have a headache? I could find you an aspirin if you like."

"No, I'm fine. How's *Mommi* Mary today?

Rebecca felt a little uncomfortable telling him his grandmother soiled herself again that morning and that she caused the old woman to cry. So instead, she told him she was napping comfortably.

Whatever had happened between the time she had arrived that morning and the present was troubling him. The way he glared at her when she spoke made her want to run and hide, but she didn't know from what. She pressed her lips together, hoping to prevent herself from spitting out some snide remark that would only add to his mood.

After wiping his mouth on a napkin, Eli walked to the back door, picked up the magazines, and said, "I have to run an errand. Can you stay until I get back?"

He didn't wait for her answer before he headed out the door. Rebecca closed her eyes just as the door slammed shut. Eli was struggling with something; she could see it in the lines around his eyes.

Rebecca couldn't speak. It wasn't that she didn't have any words. It was that she had too many, all of which would just add fuel to whatever fire was already burning in Eli's soul.

Eli's long strides marched with determination toward the barn. Rebecca wanted to run after him and find out what was bothering him. Still, the undercurrents of the past kept her planted securely to the yellow linoleum under her feet. What were all these feelings being stirred up inside of her? And what would they matter now? She made her choice a long time ago, and there was no turning back now.

***

"Rebecca?"

Mary's frail voice tumbled through the house until it reached Rebecca's ears. Pulling herself away from Eli's form, she followed Mary's call.

"Was that Eli I heard a few minutes ago? Why didn't he join us for dinner?"

Rebecca reached for Mary's hand and helped her sit up, moving her legs over the edge of the bed. "I'm not sure. He didn't say."

"That's not like him. I'd like to speak to him. Can you go get him?"

"He's running an errand. I'm sure he has already headed on his way."

Both women turned toward the window when Eli's buggy passed Mary's bedroom window on its way down the driveway.

"I'm sure he won't be long. Would you like to sit in your chair or out in the front room so you can watch the birds?"

"I wanted him to retrieve a box from the attic."

Rebecca handed Mary the quad stick and helped guide her to the front room. "I can get what you need. Tell me what I'm looking for."

"No, Eli can fetch it later."

"Suit yourself."

Rebecca sat in the rocking chair next to Mary, and both women let the steady sounds from the clock on the wall fill the silence.

"Would you like to go outside? The sun's warmed the day, and the fresh air might do you some good. I could carry a blanket out to the bench, and you could sit near the garden."

Rebecca watched Mary's face change, but she didn't answer right away. Mary's bottom lip quivered as she struggled to form a yes. When no words escaped her lips, she nodded her head instead.

Once she had Mary settled on the bench and covered her legs with a quilt, Rebecca stood and faced the years of weeds that had been left to capture the garden.

Rebecca let out her breath slowly and dropped to her knees. Hopefully, if she started to pull something that wasn't a weed, Mary would stop her. She would tug and pull on everything and anything that looked out of place until then.

Rebecca filled the wheelbarrow with so many early spring weeds and the remnants of previous gardens that they spilled over the sides within an hour. When the afternoon sun started to ascend over the rooftop, leaving Mary sitting in the shade, Rebecca helped her to her feet and led her back inside.

Mary hadn't said a word the whole time they were outside, and the long silence left Rebecca wondering if she had indeed said something to offend Mary as well. After settling Mary back in her chair, she looked out the window, hoping Eli had made it back, so she could head home. The silent treatment left her yearning to go home and away from both Bricker's for the day.

Walking through the front room on her way back to the kitchen to start supper, Rebecca heard Mary whisper, "My husband sprinkled those Johnny Jump-Up seeds in the garden the first year we moved here. They haven't bloomed in years. You pulled them all out and tossed them in the wheelbarrow with the weeds."

Rebecca's mouth flattened. "Why didn't you stop me? I don't know a flower from a weed! I didn't see any purple and yellow petals."

Mary's eyes darkened. "They hadn't bloomed yet."

When she didn't say more, Rebecca walked from the room and went to wash her hands in the kitchen sink. The strangest feeling was stirring inside of her. One of regret and sadness. It was different from the self-inflicted pain she caused herself by pushing everyone away. No, this was different. It was like nothing she'd ever felt. The agonizing betrayal of an old woman's memory was on her hands, and no amount of soap and water would wash it away.

The sun was starting to set over the horizon when Eli made it back home. Rebecca was sitting at the table working on a word search when he came in the back door.

He flipped his straw hat off and hung it on the peg as he entered. Rebecca laid her pencil aside and closed the book. "Your grandmother is already sleeping. She should be good until I return in the morning. Is there anything else you need before I leave?"

Eli moved to the sink to wash up. "I didn't unhook the buggy, so I could take you home."

"There's no need to do that. I can walk just the same."

"I didn't say you couldn't, but there's a storm rolling in, and you'll get soaking wet before you make it home."

The fire in his eyes died, and Rebecca almost felt sorry for him. Whatever was on his mind weighed heavily, and she was confident that taking her home wasn't high on his list.

She followed him out the side door and to his waiting buggy.

***

Eli studied her as she climbed inside and folded her hands neatly on her lap. He had learned way too much about what made her tick that afternoon, and it was all he could do to stop himself from lashing out at her. Eli knew better. Her sharp tongue would win against him every time if he pushed too hard. How much did he really know? Not enough for sure.

Samuel spent the better part of the morning confessing to his role in convincing him Rebecca didn't have feelings for him so many years ago. So much that it left him reliving the pain all over again. The muscle in his jaw twitched, and he snapped the reins moving his horse forward. The sudden jerk made him glance in her direction, but she kept her eyes focused ahead.

Call it compassion or plain stupidity on his part, but a small voice in the back of his mind told him to keep his thoughts to himself. It wasn't the right time. He needed to gain Rebecca's trust again before he could press her into admitting the truth. *It's up to you, Lord, isn't it? It's your will, not mine.*

***

Rebecca desperately wanted to believe the tension in the buggy had nothing to do with her. But for the life of her, she couldn't think of one thing she might have said or done to cause such an icy response. Eli clicked his tongue and called his mare by name to encourage the horse to pick up the pace. The brown topped buggy rocked back and forth in a steady response to Eli's command. The clip-clop of the horses' hooves echoed off the blacktop as dark clouds rolled overhead. When a car behind them passed too close, it made the horse pull to the side; the buggy swayed, and she voiced her concern. "Eli, what's the big hurry?"

Eli pulled in beside the Byler's Furniture Sign and stopped short of *Stitch 'n Time's* front door without barely slowing down. For years, he had hung on her every word and took every opportunity to steal a glance her way. But at that exact moment, the mere sight of her left him wondering if he really wanted to go out of his way to find the truth. But again, that small voice told him to be still.

When the buggy rolled to a stop, Rebecca waited before stepping down. She looked toward Eli and asked. "Do you want to tell me what that was all about?

He didn't move his head toward her voice but kept his eyes focused ahead. "Not now, Becca."

The deep growl of his voice told her he was in no mood to explain himself, so she stepped from the buggy and watched him pull away. No one ever called her Becca but him. But why now?

CHAPTER 7

Mary worried all day on Sunday that Rebecca wouldn't return come Monday morning. Despite how Eli tried to convince her otherwise, she didn't think she'd be back. Mary tried to read her bible to take her mind off the ill manner in which she treated Rebecca, but she couldn't concentrate on a word she read. Thank goodness it was a no church Sunday, so she had time to gather her thoughts and figure out how she would make it up to the girl.

Even Eli was in a mood that Mary couldn't explain. It was all she could do to get him to give her more than a grunt for the few questions she'd asked him that morning. Mary closed the book and rested her hand on the top of the well-worn leather binding. Not wanting to leave her alone for any longer than need be, Eli headed to the barn to check on his pregnant ewes and promised he would be back in shortly. Taking advantage of the quietness of the morning, Mary closed her eyes.

Lord, you know I've been giving myself a pity party for the last few weeks, and it's not something I've enjoyed. I know you have a plan for all of this, even though I can't see or understand what that might be. For some reason, you put Rebecca on my mind and have tasked me with helping the girl. I don't know how this old woman can help, but I'm up for the job, whatever it might be. Please give me another chance with her. It wasn't her fault she destroyed what was left of those flowers. She didn't know any better, and I should have spoken up. What is it you want me to see? And whatever is bothering Eli this morning, can you help him find peace in his troubles? Amen

When she opened her eyes, Eli was standing near her chair.

"I didn't hear you come in."

He stood staring out the window next to her chair.

Mary moved the bible to the stand, pulled up her lap blanket over her knees with her good hand, and asked, "Is something bothering you?"

"Samuel stopped by to see me yesterday morning."

"That's nice, dear. How's Emma doing?"

"Fine, I guess. He stopped to make a confession of sorts."

"A confession, that's an odd basis for a visit."

Eli sat in the rocker next to her, rested his elbows on his knees, and clasped his hands together.

"What is it, Eli?"

"I'm not really sure what to make of it, but it has to do with Rebecca. It seems she hasn't always been honest with me, and I'm not sure what I want to do about it."

"Does this have anything to do with why she stopped coming around?"

"*Jah*. And it's been so long that I'm not too sure I even want to figure it all out."

Mary waited and watched her grandson's face. Whatever Samuel had shared weighed heavy on his mind.

Eli sighed. "I don't know what to do."

Mary put a trembling hand on his arm. "Often, the best thing you can do is nothing."

"Nothing? But shouldn't I let her know what I know?"

Mary squeezed his forearm. "Would it change things now?"

"At one point, it might have. But no, not now when too much time has passed."

"Then perhaps the best thing to do is nothing."

"*Mommi*, I'm angry she lied to me."

"And she's the one who had to live with that lie all these years. I guarantee she harbors more grief from the lie than you do just finding out about it. Secrets tend to eat away at a person until they become more miserable, until the pain of hiding the truth becomes worse than the pain of revealing them."

"So, I do nothing?"

"*Jah*, nothing."

"But you don't even know what she did."

"And I don't care to know. The good Lord put that girl back in our lives for a reason. How about we stop trying to figure out why and let God work His plan like He sees fit."

"I suppose you're right."

"This time, I think I might be. Let's just pray she shows back up tomorrow."

Eli stood and picked up his grandmother's empty cup. "I'm sure Jacob won't give her any other option but to do so."

***

Anna flipped the blue shawl around her shoulders and asked again. "You sure you don't want to walk over to Emma's with me?"

Rebecca took a sip of tea. "I'm not in any mood to watch her and Samuel swoon over each other."

"Oh, Rebecca, you're exaggerating. They do no such thing."

"What do you call it then?"

Anna moved to the edge of the step. "Two people in love."

Rebecca pushed the rocker into motion with her foot. "It's sickening in my books."

"Come on, Rebecca. It would do you some good to stop in for a visit. What else are you going to do today? *Datt* and Wilma went to visit her family in Willow Brook, so you'll be here all alone."

"Suits me just fine. Maybe I'll take a walk or something. But the thoughts of spending the afternoon with Emma doesn't sound fun at all."

Rebecca noticed the eagerness in her *schwester's* eyes pleading with her to change her mind. For a moment, she felt she might weaken, but Anna bounced down the step and waved her off before she had a chance.

The early April morning gave way to pleasant temperatures. Rebecca placed her cup on the railing and followed Anna down the driveway. Anna didn't notice she was following her, even after turning into Samuel and Emma's.

Rebecca stopped at the Yoder Strawberry Acres sign. She paused only for a moment before she continued down Mystic Mill Road. She wasn't sure where she was going, but a long walk was just what she needed on such a lovely spring morning.

Thick green moss covered the north side of the trees, and the lush fields gave way to cows and sheep alike enjoying the sweet, abundant pastures of clover. The back roads of Lawrence County were quiet, and she could lose herself in her own thoughts.

Ever since Eli dropped her off the night before, her mind was fixated on his odd behavior. Between his lightning speed and the look on Mary's face after she had pulled out the row of flowers, there was an uncomfortable nagging in the pit of her stomach. Why she should care what either one of them thought was beyond her.

One step fell into another, and before she realized it, she had stopped at the white picket fence that separated Eli's sheep pasture from the barn. The barn's double doors were swung open, and she could hear the rustling of sheep and Eli's calming voice inside.

Seconds turned into minutes, and Rebecca found herself following Eli's voice in the barn. She stopped short of the gated padlock and watched as Eli had his hand inside a lambing ewe trying to turn the half-born lamb. Rebecca stepped on a paper feed sack, and the rustle alerted Eli to her presence.

He snapped his head in her direction. "I could use a hand."

Rebecca moved swiftly in his direction and dropped to her knees at the ewe's head. "Keep her calm while I try to push this lamb back inside. Its legs are in the wrong direction."

Rebecca spoke calming words in the sheep's ear and pushed its head in her lap. The ewes stomach contracted with a new wave of labor, and Eli worked to free the lamb. With a flick of his wrist, he pushed the lamb back into the birth canal and released its twisted legs. It took a few seconds for the lamb to wiggle free and fall to the floor.

Eli squeezed the lamb's nose and swung it around for the mother to lick it clean. Rebecca moved from the sheep's head and started to stand.

"Not so fast." Eli spat out. "She's not done yet."

Rebecca let the ewe tend to her lamb but stayed right by her side. With another wave, Eli checked the position of the next lamb. "Looks like this momma is having twins."

When Rebecca got too close to the new lamb, the ewe swung her head and knocked Rebecca to the floor. Eli rubbed the ewe's stomach and waited until she pushed the next lamb out on her own. "Looks like she didn't need my help this time."

Eli squeezed the new lamb's nose to open its airway, positioned the lamb next to its twin, and moved aside.

Eli stood and reached out a hand to help Rebecca to her feet. When the slime on his hand gave way, she fell back to the floor again. This time she rolled over and helped herself up.

They both moved from the stall and stood watching the ewe clean both identical white lambs. Rays of the morning sun were bouncing light off the pair, and the serenity of the scene left them speechless.

Eli moved to a bucket at the side of the stall and washed his hands. "One down, ten more to go."

"You have ten ready to lamb?"

Eli walked back to the gate and rested his foot on the bottom rung. "As far as I can tell."

"I'm glad I came along when I did. How do you do that all by yourself each time?"

"Most times, they don't need my help. They're self-sufficient. But that's a new momma, and she had me worried."

"What would have happened if you weren't there to help her out?"

"We might have lost the lambs or the ewe and the lambs. The next couple of weeks will be busy around here with lambing season. I'll be staying pretty close to the barn as much as I can."

"Well, I guess it's good I'm here to help you with Mary then, isn't it?"

Eli nodded his head once and moved to the next stall to check on another ewe. Without looking her way, Eli asked, "Did you need something?"

Rebecca brushed the straw off her blue dress and replied, "No, I was out for a walk and heard you in here. It was more me being nosy than anything else."

"Rebecca Byler, nosy? I would have never guessed."

"Is that a hint of sarcasm I detect?"

"Call it what you may, but if I know one thing about you, it's that you like to be in everyone else's business. But you don't like anyone else in yours. Isn't that right, Becca?"

Heat rose from her shoulders to the top of her head. Not because he called her on the table about her nosiness, but because he called her Becca again.

She hadn't moved from her stance at the gate when he moved back past her. When he stopped at her shoulder, he whispered in her ear. "I'm bound and determined to figure you out. I won't be lied to so easily this time."

The rueful look on Eli's face was warning enough. What happened next left her gasping for breath. He reached up and pulled a loose hair that had escaped her *kapp* and in a raspy voice, said, "Fool me once, shame on you, fool me twice, shame on me."

He moved from her side and walked to the house. After he was far enough away, she exhaled as she watched him move across the yard. Her heart pounded, and she couldn't fathom what he was referring to. She had told herself and him so many lies over the years that she couldn't be sure which one he might be referring to. But it really didn't matter because every one of them was to protect him. One secret led to another, which led to a lie. The vicious cycle continued for years until he finally gave up on her and any hope they had for a future. After a few minutes, Rebecca left the barn and headed toward home.

Everything felt like it was spinning out of control. For years, she'd been able to keep everyone at arm's length for fear her true shame would be revealed. But the run-in she just had with Eli left her shaken. Why suddenly, and what did Eli know?

The warm sun on Rebecca's shoulders did little to calm her nerves. When she made it to Emma and Samuel's driveway, she stood at the end and tried to figure out how to speak to Samuel alone. He was the only other person in Willow Springs that had any idea what tormented her. But speaking to him alone without Emma present would be highly unlikely.

When Anna and Emma saw her standing near the mailbox, they hollered in unison. "Rebecca, come join us."

It was too late to go unseen, so she followed their voices to Emma's front porch. Anna was the first to notice her shaken state. "Are you okay? You look like you have the weight of the world on your shoulders."

Rebecca looked over her shoulder toward the barn. "Is Samuel around?"

Emma pointed across the road to her *bruder,* Daniel's. "Why would you need to speak to Samuel?"

Rebecca shuddered. "I ... I have a question about ... well, never mind, it can wait for another day."

Emma furrowed her eyebrows together. "I'm sure he won't mind you stopping over at Daniel's if it's something important."

"Perhaps I'll do that. Thank you."

Anna stood and moved an empty chair closer to hers. "Are you in a hurry? Would you like to have a glass of Meadow Tea with us? Mint in the garden is coming in fast and Emma made a fresh batch yesterday. It's about as good as *Mamm's* was."

"No, I don't think so. I best go ask Samuel my question and get home. I feel a headache coming on, and I'd like to take a nap."

Rebecca prayed all the way to Daniel's that she would be able to catch Samuel alone long enough to ask him about Eli.

***

Daniel pulled a stool up to the workbench and took his English Bible from its hiding spot behind his toolbox. "So, how did it go with Eli yesterday?"

Samuel took his Sunday wool hat off and brushed his bangs off his forehead. "About as well as I expected. He was shocked that I played along with her for as long as I did. I wished I could tell him the whole story, but I have to trust Rebecca will come to her senses one of these days and go to the Lord with her confession."

Looking down at the bible, Daniel turned to the place they had left off the week before and waited until Samuel finished.

"I'm almost sure Eli will be joining us soon for our study. Just as I suspected, his liberal upbringing in Lancaster allowed a more in-depth study of God's word. I think he will be a great addition to our time together."

Daniel shifted on the stool. "I suspected he had a better understanding of scripture than he let on."

"*Jah*, I didn't ask too many questions. He was more concerned with understanding why Rebecca was so set on making him believe we were courting than anything else."

Daniel rubbed the short beard on his chin with one hand. "That makes two of us, I guess. I don't understand it myself."

"It's a long story and one only Rebecca can tell. But I took care of my part in it, and now we have to wait and see how long Rebecca will carry the rest of the burden herself."

Samuel patted the open bible. "Before we get started, tell me how you made out with the Kauffman boys."

Daniel propped his elbow on the table and began. "Just as we suspected, they've been visiting the Mennonite Church in town on our no church Sunday. Word is spreading through the younger members of the district, just like we prayed."

Samuel looked toward the door when he thought he heard a sound. When nothing else alerted his attention, he continued, "I spoke to Emma last week about what this might mean for us. If the bishop and the ministers, especially her father, get word of us studying the English Bible, we'll all be shunned."

Daniel tilted his ear toward the door and put his finger to his lip to quiet Samuel. He walked to the entrance of the tack shop and opened the door. "Must be one of the barn cats making a ruckus."

Once Daniel retook his seat, Samuel added, "Eli is a crucial player. He's been reading God's word a lot longer than I have, and he will be a good influence on some of the younger men in the community."

"I'd like to say I had an influence, but with being raised English, I think you or Eli have a better chance in convincing the men to be open to what we want to teach them."

"*Jah*, I think you're right. More and more of the younger people want to know more beyond the three-hour service on Sunday morning. They are thirsty for Jesus, and I want to show them that being a Christian means more than following a set of rules handed down from generation to generation. God wants so much more from us."

Daniel stood and walked to the door again when a noise drew his attention back to the central part of the shop. "So, how is Emma making out with reaching out to some of the younger women?"

"The bakery is the perfect cover. She is cautious with whom she speaks and keeps things to a particular age group. The bishop doesn't realize it, but hopefully, by the time they find out what we're up to, we will have enough families ready to break off from our Old Order and start a New Order."

Daniel pulled the door closed. "You do realize that the bishop is going to blame this all on the English kid turned Amish."

Samuel slapped Daniel on the shoulder. "I'm sure of it. But don't worry, we're in this together. If one falls, we all fall. But in my books, if we are falling in the name of Jesus, we are doing precisely what God instructs us to do."

***

Rebecca held her hand over her mouth as she crouched down behind a stack of strawberry baskets listening to their conversation. What on earth were they up to, and what were they doing talking to people about Jesus? Didn't they know they'd be put in the *bann* if the bishop ever found out?

She knew her *schwester* and Samuel were up to something, but she never dreamed it would involve going against their ways this far. Forget talking to Samuel about Eli. As much as she could tell, Eli had a stake in the matter as well.

How dare Eli talk to her about secrets. By the sounds of it, he had a few hidden away as well.

CHAPTER 8

R ebecca tossed and turned all night with the thought of facing Eli. Would he press her more, and would she be able to hold her tongue on what she overheard in the barn? Before taking off to Mary's, she stopped into *Stitch 'n Time* to check on Anna.

Anna was out the door and in the shop long before Rebecca had come downstairs. Wilma and their father had left early for town, so she grabbed a biscuit and headed to find her *schwester*.

The shop door was propped open, and the tangy smell of vinegar and cooked spinach filled the air. A propane burner on the porch had a big pot of freshly chopped spinach simmering. A tub near the steps held a vat of fiber soaking in a vinegar and water solution. Rebecca popped a bit of biscuit in her mouth and pushed the fiber underneath the water.

"How long has this been soaking?"

Anna waved her away. "I've got it under control. I know how long it takes."

Rebecca nodded her head in the direction of the simmering pot of fresh greens. "You'll want to make sure you keep the time on both the dye and vinegar solution. If you make a few batches, you want to ensure the color lot stays the same. Measure things precisely, so you get the same dye lot for each batch."

Anna pushed her away from the pan. "Aren't you going to be late?"

"A few minutes here or there isn't going to make a bit of difference."

Rebecca stepped in the shop and pulled the ledger book out from under the counter. "Are you keeping good records?"

"For heaven's sake, Rebecca, you've only been gone a couple days. I believe I'm more than capable of taking care of the shop in your absence. I've recorded everything down to the last penny." Anna pulled the black leather book from Rebecca's hand and put it back under the counter. "Now get out of here. You're in my way."

Rebecca moved about the storeroom and pointed to an almost empty hook. "You'll need to pick up some purple cabbage and work on dyeing more of this color. You know how the *Englishers* love pink."

Anna moved toward her *schwester,* took her by the arm, and directed her to the door. "I don't need you second-guessing my ability; now go. *Datt* put me in charge of the shop, and I'll run things as I see fit."

Rebecca grabbed the door frame. "But let me help you strain that pot of spinach, then I'll be on my way."

"*Nee,* I've got it. What you can do …is talk to Eli about buying more raw wool. I bet he'll start shearing soon and we'll need to get our order in. We certainly aren't going to have enough with our four alpacas." She pointed to a basket near the wall. "That's the last vat of fiber we have from last year's shearing."

Both women walked to the porch, and Anna lifted the lid from the simmering pot and used the wooden spoon to check the depth of color. "This should make a nice spring color to add to our line."

Rebecca peered in the pot. "I think you need to boil it down some more. And don't forget to record the time. Boil all batches the exact amount of time."

"Would you please just go and quit telling what I already know."

"All right already. I'm going."

Rebecca skipped down the steps and hollered over her shoulder. "Don't forget to order a crate of red cabbage from The Mercantile."

Anna raised her hand and waved her off before getting back to work dyeing the last of the white alpaca fiber. It was easy to convince Rebecca she was doing fine, especially with no customers in the shop. But her hands were sweating. Let alone the uneasiness creeping up her chest. The mere thought of turning the open sign around left her gasping for air.

***

Eli sat at the kitchen table, enjoying the last few sips of coffee when Rebecca tapped on the side door and let herself in. He couldn't keep his annoyance from his tone when she showed up over an hour late. He had work to do and tending to his grandmother's personal needs kept him from checking on a few missing sheep.

"Good morning." His disgruntled response didn't faze her. Moving to the stove, she poured herself a cup of coffee before leaning back on the counter and bringing the steaming mug to her mouth.

"Take a seat, Becca."

Something about the way he said Becca made her cringe. But she took a seat and waited for him to gather his thoughts.

He cleared his throat and set his coffee cup aside. "I do believe when I hired you, we agreed you would get here in plenty of time to get Mary up and ready for the day. I have a herd of missing sheep, and your tardiness kept me from my work."

"It's just an hour! Don't you think you're being a bit dramatic?"

Eli sucked in a breath through his nose, and his chest puffed up like a strutting rooster. "The point is, I expect you to be here when you say you will. No, ifs, ands, or buts about it."

Rebecca picked up his cup and carried it to the sink. "Okay, okay, I get it. It won't happen again."

Eli stood and pushed his chair in harder than necessary. "*Mommi* Mary wants you to wake her at precisely nine o'clock. You are to bring that notebook and pencil to her room and be ready to take notes."

She sipped her coffee and raised her eyebrows at his strange request. "Take notes for what?"

"I'm not sure, but she has something she wants to get down on paper, and you're going to help her do it."

Rebecca stayed quiet for a long moment as he watched her wheels turn. No doubt she was trying to find an excuse, any excuse to deny his request. She was treading on thin ice, and he hoped she wouldn't test him more.

He steadied his eyes on her for a few moments longer than usual. She had disappointed him in so many ways. Still, a twinge of longing edged in between the layers of past mistakes. Why did her eyes have to awaken something he thought he'd gotten over?

Seeing her mouth tighten, he added, "I may need your help this afternoon."

She rinsed her cup and set it upside down on the drainboard. "Is that in my job duties?"

He had the feeling that she was baiting him into another battle of wills, but instead of responding, he opened the door and headed to the barn.

***

At nine o'clock, Rebecca carried a tray of tea to Mary's room and lightly knocked on the door before opening it.

With the notebook tucked under her arm, she set the tray down on the dresser before going to Mary's bedside.

Rebecca laid her hand on Mary's shoulder and gently shook her. "Eli said you wanted me to wake you at nine."

Mary opened her eyes but didn't move. "I was having the sweetest dream."

"Do you want me to come back later?"

"*Nee*, I want you to help me sit up."

Rebecca helped her to a sitting position and reached for the brush. She pulled it through Mary's thin, waist-length gray hair. After brushing the knots out, she parted it down the middle and coiled it up tight to the back of her head, covering it with a *kapp*.

"Would you like to get out of your nightdress?"

A frown flickered across her face. "I suppose not. That would require too much energy, and I best keep all my strength for what I have planned for us today."

"Eli told me you have some things you want to get down on paper. I brought in the notebook and pen like you asked."

"Good. We will get started in a few minutes. How about you pour us a cup of tea first."

"I brewed a pot of Earl Grey. Will that do?"

"It will."

Rebecca watched the old woman out of the corner of her eye and half suspected she was trying to work up to something.

Mary blew over the rim of her cup. "Tell me what happened between you and Eli."

Rebecca stiffened her shoulders. "I do believe that's between Eli and me."

Mary raised her eyebrows. "Well, let's get something straight starting right here and now. The good Lord laid you on my heart, and we are to share this season together for some reason. Starting right here, right now."

Rebecca's heart drummed in her ears, and she sat still for a few seconds. Why on earth was Mary suddenly interested?

"I'm not sure what you are referring to, but I still don't see any reason to bring up the past."

Why should she feel guilty of something that happened so long ago? But the way Mary asked her to explain left her scrambling for a logical answer. *So what if she pushed Eli away with a lie. What did it matter now?*

Mary handed Rebecca her cup and pointed to the notebook laying on the bed. Rebecca tried to change the subject. "So, what is it you want me to write down for you?"

Mary's eyes narrowed slightly, but she said nothing.

"Eli said you wanted me to record something for you?"

Mary sighed softly, looking weary. "I want to tell someone my story before it's lost. Forever buried in my grave so deep my son Andy will never know the truth."

Mary's eyes took on a look of regret. One moment she was bold and direct about demanding Rebecca tell her about Eli, and the next, her face took on a deep pain, just dying to be released. Rebecca was confused at the array of emotions the old woman displayed.

Rebecca picked up the notebook. "I will do my best."

Mary stiffened at Rebecca's statement. "I'm sure you will. But this will be a journey for both of us. What you will soon learn will be hard for you to comprehend, but I am trusting you to write my words in such a way that there will be no doubt Andy will understand the magnitude of his past."

Rebecca tilted her head in Mary's direction, almost unsure she wanted to walk through this journey with her. While she was intrigued by the secret Mary alluded to, she could feel herself being drawn into revealing more of herself than she was comfortable doing.

Rebecca crossed her legs and balanced the notebook on her knee. "Where would you like to start?"

"With you answering my first question. What happened between you and Eli?"

"Mary, again, I don't think that is any of your concern."

Mary tilted her head and whispered, "But you see, my dear, it has everything to do with where we need to start."

Heat surged into Rebecca's cheeks. "I'm not going there. And besides, it's your story you want to tell, not mine."

In a more serious tone than Rebecca had ever heard come out of Mary's mouth, she said, "Confession is risky. I'm not blinded by the mask you've been wearing around Eli for years."

Mary rubbed her useless hand and took in a calming breath. "The only way to completely and utterly trust another person is to share some of your darkest moments. I'm about to share things with you that I've only told one other person, and I have to know that you can be trusted."

"Trusted with what?" Rebecca asked.

"With a series of events that will change my son's life forever. It's the one thing I can leave him; an explanation."

"How is me telling you what happened with Eli going to change a thing?"

"Because I'm here to show you that even the darkest secrets can turn bright. That some people's worst mistakes can turn into a beacon of hope for others."

Rebecca rubbed her temple and shook her head. "Mary, you're talking in circles. I have no idea what you're trying to tell me."

Mary sat taller. "Think about this. When you're trapped by secrecy, you don't want the advice of people who have never walked in your shoes. You want someone who has been where you've walked and made it back alive. That person is me. That's why I'm pushing you to confide in me. You need to know that I walked in the murky waters of denial and self-loathing, much like I've seen in you over the last few years."

Mary looked out the window and took a few minutes before continuing. "I wasted many years pushing my husband away, fearing he wouldn't understand the depth of my despair. He often said all it would take was time to heal all things. But when I was in the midst of it, I wouldn't allow myself to believe it."

Mary's expression grew serious. "Perhaps you can start recording my words later. I've become quite tired all of the sudden." She laid her head back on her pillow and closed her eyes.

Rebecca sat still for a few minutes, waiting to be dismissed, only to hear her labored breathing take on a soft snore.

She laid the notebook on the dresser, still void of any words, and retreated to the kitchen.

The clock on the living room wall chimed ten, and she sat at the table trying to make sense of the rambling words of the old woman. *What was all that about? Half of what she said seemed more like a riddle than anything that made a bit of sense.*

Everything was so confusing. Eli's mumbled warning about once a fool, to Samuel and Daniel's secret bible study, and now Mary's cryptic message left her senses on edge.

She picked up the basket of laundry she had gathered earlier and headed to the basement. Sorting the darks from the whites, Rebecca picked up one of Eli's Sunday white shirts and brought it to her nose. *What a strange thing to do*, she thought. His musky smell tickled her nose, and she quickly dropped it back in the basket.

"Becca, are you down there?"

"*Jah*, what is it?"

"I could really use a hand in the barn."

Before she had a chance to answer, the screen door slammed. She turned off the washing machine, ran up the steps, and rushed to follow Eli across the yard and into one of the gated pens.

"I'm afraid we are going to lose this young ewe. My hand is way too big to turn this lamb. I'm going to need you to reach inside and do it.

"Me? You want me to turn the lamb?"

"*Jah*, we don't have much time. Your hand is much smaller than mine. I will keep her calm, and I'll walk you through it."

Eli quickly tied an apron around Rebecca's blue dress and pointed to the floor. "You'll need to get your footing in case she kicks. Steady yourself on one knee and lean into her belly."

"I don't know if I can do this; what if I hurt her?"

"It's either we turn the lamb and help her deliver it, or we lose both the ewe and the lamb."

Rebecca took each one of Eli's instructions and performed it with care. The young ewe was clearly tired and gave Rebecca little resistance. When Eli told Rebecca to wait until a natural contraction began again, she took in a deep breath. She exhaled loudly like she was in labor herself. Rebecca pulled the lamb from the mother's womb with one swift push and squeezed its nose to remove the mucus, just like she had seen Eli do the other day. She moved the lamb to its mother's nose and moved away so the ewe could lick it clean.

Rebecca fell back on her heels. "Oh, my goodness. That was intense."

Eli stood and reached his hand out to help Rebecca stand. "It typically is. This is the first year I've had to help many young ewes deliver. Normally I'm a pesky standby to nature's natural rhythm."

"Why are so many having issues?"

"Mere numbers, I'm sure. I've grown the herd this year, so it's just the fact that there are more lambing."

They backed out of the pen and leaned on the gate, watching the mother take to her baby. "How many more will lamb?"

"It's hard to tell. But at least a dozen or so. Hopefully, by May, we should see the pastures filled with lambs, and I can start shearing in June and July."

"Speaking of shearing, have you given any more thought to Anna and I buying raw fiber from you? I know you've contracted with a fiber wholesaler for the bulk of it. Still, we would really like to promote our yarn being supplied locally."

"It depends."

Rebecca looked his way and asked, "Depends on what?"

"How much help I can get with shearing."

"You want me to help?"

"I suppose if you want the best of the lot, you best be right in the midst of it."

"I don't know the first thing about shearing sheep."

"Who shears your alpacas?"

"We've always hired someone to come do it for us."

"Well then, I guess you have a choice to make. You can continue to hire someone to shear your alpacas and buy your raw fiber from a sheep farmer you don't know. Or you can learn how to shear them yourself. I'd say you'd want to cut the middle-man out of the picture as best as you can."

His expression altered. "So, what do you think? Are you up to learning how to be a sheep farmer?"

Rebecca tilted her head in his direction and added, "So let me get this straight. You want me to care for your grandmother, cook your meals, wash your clothes, and now you want me to add sheep shearing to my list of duties. Oh, and let me add being your grandmother's memoir writer to the list."

He looked at her again and shook his head. "If that's not enough, I can hand you off some of my chores as well."

"I think I have plenty if you don't mind. This certainly isn't what I signed up for." She made a loud TSK sound, sighed, and left him standing in the barn.

CHAPTER 9

Rebecca carried the clothes basket to the side yard and watched Eli out of the corner of her eye while she hung rows of blue and black. He had rolled up his shirt sleeves and fixed the fence close to the road. The post driver he was using to hammer in a new fence post bounced off the metal, making a series of precisely timed clangs ring through the air. The sight left her having a hard time turning her face from the scene.

Walking around the side of the house, she stepped over a cluster of tulips before heading inside. The warm sunshine was drying out the soggy ground, and she couldn't help but try to envision what Mary's gardens once looked like.

Something was changing with her, but she couldn't quite put her finger on it. In the four days she had spent at Eli and Mary's, she found herself caring more about Mary than herself.

On the other hand, Eli still drove her crazy, but there was a softness she felt anytime he came to mind.

What was it she was feeling? A calmness, a belonging, a hope for the future? Could she really think time could heal all things like Mary said?

Pushing the screen door open, she stepped inside the kitchen to find Mary sitting at the table.

"You should have waited for me to help you."

"I might not get around as well as I used to, but so far, I can still find my way to the table, even if it does take me twice as long."

"Still, you should have waited until I came back inside."

"No sense in worrying about it now. I'm here, and I can stay right in this seat until after dinner. I'd like to get some writing done if you have time later."

"Rebecca, sometimes I wonder…"

"What's that?"

"If maybe we could bring my garden back."

"I don't know the first thing about gardening." Rebecca lifted her hands in the air. "Hence pulling out all your flowers last week."

Rebecca let out a raspy chuckle. "Emma got all the green thumbs in the family."

Mary snorted. "Perhaps we could at least clean up the porch and wash the windows."

Groaning inwardly, Rebecca asked, "What do you want me to do first? Fix dinner, clean the porch, or help you get your thoughts on paper?"

"I suppose we have been asking you to do a good bit around here. It's just that this old house has needed a young woman's touch for a good long time."

Rebecca mumbled under her breath, "Lucky me."

"What was that dear?"

"Nothing."

Rebecca moved to the stove, pulled the casserole out of the oven, and placed it in the center of the table. It was a good thing *Mamm* taught her to cook; she could at least keep them fed if she couldn't bring Mary's gardens back to life.

She moved to the back porch and rang the dinner bell. Eli was nowhere in sight, but she was confident the sound would lure him to the house.

Within minutes, he was at the sink telling his grandmother about the three new lambs and what a great help Rebecca had been.

Rebecca stifled her irritation. She shook her head and thought. *What's the matter with me? He was trying to give me a compliment, and all I could think about was the list of chores he kept giving me.*

Dinner was all but a blur to Rebecca as she tried to stop the conversation in her head. Eli and Mary were in their own little world, trying to pull her in every chance they got. It was like a raging war taking place inside with nowhere to retreat but further inside herself.

She didn't understand how Eli could act like he didn't mind her around when she had done nothing but discourage him in the five years she'd known him. And then Mary, how could she still be smiling after a stroke took every ounce of dignity the woman had left? For goodness' sake, the poor woman couldn't even go to the bathroom herself. Something was different between the two of them, but what was it? Maybe she could figure it out once she started writing Mary's story. Perhaps then she could figure out what made the two of them tick.

Eli leaned back in his chair and patted his stomach. "Thanks for the meal, but I best get back to work."

Mary lifted her limp arm on the table and rubbed her gnarled fingertips with her good hand. "Rebecca's going to clean the porch and wash the front windows this afternoon."

Eli grabbed his straw hat off the peg by the back door. "*Jah*, I'd been meaning to do that. But there's never been enough time in the day for such things." The screen door bounced behind him.

Rebecca didn't respond to his comment and gathered the plates and silverware from the table and carried them to the sink. "Do you want me to help you to the living room while I clean up the kitchen?"

"No, I think I'd like to sit right here until you're finished."

"Suit yourself."

Rebecca made a mental note of everything she needed to get done before heading home. Thank goodness Wilma took care of running the Byler house now, or she'd have a full day's work to do once she returned home. She ran her hands under the warm water and thought. *I guess Datt marrying her didn't turn out so bad after all. Oh, my gosh! There I go again. Where are these thoughts coming from?*

Rebecca pulled a bucket from beneath the sink and two rags to tackle the front window and rocking chairs on the porch. A layer of winter grime covered the white rockers, and a film covered the front windowpanes.

Mary settled herself comfortably in the chair near the window. "Thank you. Now I'll be able to make sure you get all the streaks."

"You're welcome," she said through gritted teeth and went to work sweeping dead leaves off the covered porch. The half-smile on Mary's face warmed her heart as she tackled cleaning the windows. After getting most of the dirt cleaned from the two identical rockers, Rebecca returned inside. "Would you like to sit outside for a spell?"

Mary's lopsided smile said all she needed to hear, and she helped the woman move outside. "Bring me the notebook, would you?"

Rebecca tucked a lap blanket around Mary's knees and returned after the pen and paper.

After she settled in the chair beside her, she asked, "So, what is it you want me to take notes on?"

Mary stared off in the distance and then pointed to the maple tree at the edge of the property. "See that tree over there? My husband planted it the week we arrived in Willow Springs. That was sixty-five years ago."

Rebecca looked at the tree and gave a curious nod. "Do you want me to write that down?"

"*Nee*, I'm just remembering that's all."

Rebecca tapped the pen on the notebook. "I'm not trying to be difficult, but I'm not sure what you want from me."

"Patience, child. Give this old woman a chance to gather her thoughts. The story I need you to record spans back some sixty-plus years, and it will take me a little bit to get my facts straight. I mustn't leave anything out."

Rebecca let the seconds turn into minutes as she waited for Mary to begin. Inpatient as she was, she couldn't wait a minute longer before she asked, "What was your husband like?"

"Noah was a good man," Mary said firmly. He had a big heart and cared about many things. He was just …quiet."

Rebecca wrote down Mary's exact words. "Did you court long before you married?"

Mary took in a long breath and closed her eyes as if a painful memory surfaced too close for comfort. "*Nee*."

"So, was it love, at first sight?"

Again, Mary sighed. "Perhaps it was for him and his first love. But not for me."

Rebecca clicked the pen. "I'm confused. Did Noah love another before you?"

"Not before me, but despite me."

"If he didn't love you, why did he ask you to marry him?"

"All in good time. I need to start from the beginning not in the middle for it to make sense."

Rebecca made a small note on the side of the paper to go back and ask Mary the question again when she felt it might fit into her story. "Where do you want to start?"

Mary opened her eyes and boldly replied, "1944"

"What happened in 1944?"

"My father went to France to serve in a hospital during World War II."

Rebecca let out a small gasp. "Your father served in the military? How is that so?"

"He felt the Lord was leading him to serve our troops in France right after D-day. My father had a servant's heart, and he knew he couldn't fight in the war, so he volunteered to work in the field hospital."

"But where did that leave you? You couldn't have been more than thirteen or fourteen in 1944."

"I was thirteen to be exact, and he left me with his best friend and neighbor, Amos Bricker. Eli's Great-Grandfather."

"What happened then?"

Mary pulled the quilt tight on her lap. "The Japanese bombed Pearl Harbor, and my father was gone for over a year."

Rebecca wrote down Mary's response and leaned in closer. "Were you scared for him?"

"I loved my *datt*. It was just him and me for so long I was beside myself with worry. I wasn't sure if I'd ever see him again. My mother died having me, so my father was all the family I ever had."

"I don't understand why you want to write this all down. Doesn't Eli and his family already know all of this?"

"They only know bits and pieces, and I need to set things straight."

"Were you mad your father left you behind to go support the troops? How did that go over with your district in Lancaster? Wasn't serving in the military frowned upon, much like it is here?"

"At the time, I understood he felt God calling him to help, and I loved him for his dedication. After almost eight months of worrying that he wouldn't return, I realized there were things much worse than my father not coming home from war."

"But he did come home, right?"

"He did, but life was never the same once he returned."

Rebecca scurried to catch up with Mary's words while the old woman wiped the moisture from her eyes.

Rebecca positioned her pen and asked, "Why were things not the same? Did he get hurt?"

"Physically hurt? No. Emotionally devastated? Yes."

"How so?"

Mary rubbed her limp arm. "I think I've had enough for one day. Perhaps I should go lie down for a spell."

Rebecca was disappointed by Mary's lack of energy to continue with the story. It was just starting to get good, and she was dying to see what was so emotionally devastating for Mary's father.

Rebecca laid the notebook and pen aside and helped Mary stand to move inside.

***

After setting a pot of vegetable beef soup on the stove's warming burner, she proceeded outside to tell Eli she was leaving.

The afternoon sun had already receded behind the barn, and the cool spring breeze whipped around the open door and under her skirt. She pushed the hem of her blue dress back down and stepped in out of the wind.

"Eli?"

"Back here." She followed his voice to the back of the barn and into the tack shop. He stood at his workbench, sharpening a pair of shearers.

He tipped his head in her direction. "Done for the day?"

"*Jah*, I left a pot of soup on the stove for you both."

"*Denki*."

Rebecca leaned up against the door frame and asked, "Have you ever talked to your grandmother about her father?"

"Not too much. She keeps a lot of her past under lock and key. Why do you ask?"

"I think something traumatic happened to her when she was younger. She started to tell me about your grandfather going to

France to help in World War II, but she got tired, and we quit for the day."

Eli sat down on a stool and ran the blade over a sharpening stone he moved with a pedal on the floor. "I've asked my mother if she knew anything, but what she does know, she wasn't too keen on sharing with me."

"What do you know about your grandfather Noah?"

"I only met him once."

Rebecca pulled her chin to her chest. "You only met your grandfather once?"

"We didn't visit much. When he was fifteen, my father left Willow Springs to work on my Great-Grandfather Bricker's dairy farm. By the time I came along, he had already taken over the daily operation, and it left us little time to visit."

"Didn't your grandmother ever go back to Lancaster?"

"Nope, not that I knew of. For that matter, I don't think they were ever invited to come visit us."

"That's a shame."

"It's just how it was, I guess."

Rebecca studied him from her spot near the door. When Eli stopped to test the blade's sharpness, he looked her way. Rebecca saw something in his expression that made her want to stay. Perhaps her probing questions gave him reason to share what he knew with someone who might be interested in what he had to say.

Rebecca's mouth tightened. "Why do you think your father wouldn't want his parents to visit? You would think they would like their sons to know their grandparents."

Eli blew sharpening dust off the blade and said, "My *datt* was more concerned with getting the best milk price than making sure his *kinner* knew anything about their family heritage."

She crossed her arms over her chest, pondering his reply.

Eli laid the knife on the bench. "I suppose he did the best he could, considering the circumstances."

"What circumstances?"

"My *datt's* uncles were furious that my great-grandfather would leave the farm to his grandson and not them. It always put a real wedge between any family dynamics the Bricker family had."

"TSK. TSK."

Eli glared in her direction after her judgmental response.

"I'm sorry. I didn't mean any slight against your father. I guess I just don't understand, I might not always agree with my

151

own father, but he made sure we knew our extended family as best as we could."

"No offense taken. The way I see it, maybe you'll discover the big secret that has plagued this family for years. I'm too close to the situation, and I only get frustrated by the lame excuses I'm thrown. Besides, my *datt* and I aren't on the best of terms. He was furious when I moved to Willow Springs to take care of *Mommi* Mary. He felt I had a responsibility to him and the legacy of Bricker Farms."

"And you didn't?"

"You know how it works. The farm goes to the youngest son. I was the oldest, and my hopes of a future in the Bricker Dairy Farm fell way down the line for me."

"Then why did he get so upset when you moved to Willow Springs?"

Eli picked up his straw hat and brushed it across his thigh before putting it back on his head. "Perhaps you'll help me figure that all out by recording whatever *Mommi* has on her mind."

Rebecca let him pass her in the door frame and followed him through the barn, stopping at the pen where the young ewe was nursing her lamb. "Looks like she took to her baby fine."

Eli rested his elbows on the gate. "I'd say it was a good day all around."

"I better be heading home."

Eli followed her outside. "Do you want a ride?"

She waved over her shoulder and headed to the road. "*Nee*, I can make it home before it gets dark."

***

The mystery Mary started to unravel was playing havoc in Rebecca's head. What on earth would force Eli's grandfather to marry his grandmother unless he was in love with her? She'd heard of arranged marriages before. Could that be what happened? Did her father already arrange for her to marry Noah long before he left for the war? Or was it something else? She could hardly wait to return to Mary's story the next day.

Picking up the pace of her twenty-minute walk, she played every scenario over in her mind. What was so important that Mary needed to tell her story now? And why was Eli's father so upset that he chose to come to northwestern Pennsylvania when there was no hope for him to take over the farm. It only made sense that Eli came here to help Mary. She had no one else. Something just didn't add up, and her inquisitive mind was working overtime trying to make sense of it all.

Rebecca couldn't wait to get home and tell Anna all she'd learned that day. But even before she could figure out where to start, her conscience caught up to her, and she decided it wasn't her story to tell. Again, her day at Mary and Eli's was something she didn't want to share with anyone. It was like they were letting her into their world, and she liked being part of something outside of the Byler household for some unknown reason.

CHAPTER 10

It was all Rebecca could do to get out of the house and to Eli's on time the following day. She practically ran all the way to his farm and stepped into the kitchen, out of breath.

Eli glanced at the clock on the wall and covered his bible with a newspaper. "So, I see you do know how to tell time after all."

Rebecca removed the blue scarf from her head and hung it on the hook near the door. After rearranging her *kapp* and smoothing a wrinkle from her skirt, she moved to the stove.

Picking up a bowl of eggs, she cracked a few in another bowl and asked, "Is Mary awake?"

"She hasn't hollered for me yet. Perhaps she's waiting for you. She's getting pretty particular about hanging on until you're here to help."

"Let me go check on her real quick."

Eli waited until she had made her way into the other room before he moved the English bible to the top of the hutch at the side of the room. The last thing he needed was for Rebecca to catch him reading such a version. He needed to get to the bottom of many things with her but sharing his private bible studies wasn't high on his priority list quite yet.

Rebecca stopped at Mary's door and looked over her shoulder into the kitchen. She watched as Eli placed a book on the top of the cabinet. Curious, she thought. *Why would he hide his bible from her? Unless it had something to do with what she overheard Samuel and Daniel talking about. Just one more thing she needed to get to the bottom of.*

***

Mary sat on the edge of the bed, hair askew and feeling forlorn. A ray of sun shone in through her window, bouncing a rainbow of colors off a glass of water sitting on her nightstand. How many years had she sat on the edge of the same bed, looking forward to another day? Lately, each passing day seemed longer than the next, and she fought harder each day to keep a lighthearted outlook.

Without taking her eyes from the window, she mumbled, "What day is it?"

Rebecca moved to her side. "It's Tuesday, April twelfth." Letting out a small giggle, Rebecca added. "Do you have somewhere you need to be today?"

Mary didn't answer but thought. *How had old age caught up to me so quickly? Seems just like yesterday I had enough energy for ten women. Now I can't even go pee by myself.* She felt a wave of grumpiness overcome her, but pushed it aside.

Giving up every ounce of her independence was heart-wrenching. Even after Noah died, she found peace and solitude by spending time with God in her garden. Now she couldn't even do that. She dropped her head and closed her eyes.

Rebecca stooped down to her level. "Are you feeling ill?"

Mary looked around the room as if she were looking for someone. "Noah, did he go to the barn already? I haven't made his breakfast yet."

Rebecca's blank stare, along with her voice taking on a high octave, alarmed Mary when she asked, "Noah?"

She looked up into the girl's green and brown flecked eyes. For a moment, she couldn't place her name. The rising sun added a halo around her head, and she had trouble remembering her name. Tears unexpectedly pooled on her bottom lashes.

"I'll be right back. Let me go get Eli."

As soon as Rebecca left the room, Mary wiped the moisture from her face, and things became clear.

Within a few minutes, Eli sat on the edge of her bed. "*Mommi*, are you feeling all right? Rebecca said you were asking about grandfather."

Mary patted Eli's arm. "Don't mind the ramblings of this old woman. I just got confused for a minute."

Eli looked over at Rebecca and shrugged his shoulders.

"Now go and get out of here. You have sheep to tend to, and Rebecca and I have things to do."

Eli walked out of the room and motioned for Rebecca to follow him. "What was that all about?"

Rebecca whispered, "I have no idea, but she clearly thought your grandfather was still living. And I swear she didn't know who I was for a minute."

"How about you get her ready for the day, and I'll go start breakfast."

Rebecca looked over her shoulder into Mary's room. "Let's not confuse her anymore than we have to. If she sees you in the kitchen, she'll really be out of sorts. Go to the barn, and I'll ring the bell when I have breakfast on the table."

Rebecca didn't know what to think of Mary's odd behavior. But she went about taking care of her personal needs and sat her at the table right next to Eli's chair while she finished breakfast.

***

After breakfast, Rebecca brought out the notebook and sat down beside Mary. "Do you feel up to telling more of your story?"

Mary tipped her head and gave Rebecca a strange look. "It will take God to change your heart."

Confused at Mary's odd statement, she pointed to the notebook. "Do you want me to write that down?"

Mary continued without answering. "A heart change will mean a transformed life."

Rebecca picked up her pen and scrambled to write down Mary's comments.

Mary's bottom lip started to quiver. "My father was furious with me."

Rebecca crossed her legs and pulled the lined paper closer. "How so?"

"I embarrassed him."

"By doing what? Because you married Noah?"

"I was a little girl when he left for the war. I was a woman when he returned."

"But why would that embarrass him? Time doesn't standstill. It was bound to happen."

"But not the way he had envisioned it."

"I don't understand. I'm getting confused. If you want me to record things, I have to understand what it is you're trying to explain."

Rebecca flipped back through the notes she had taken the day before. "Let's start where we ended off yesterday. You had just told me that your father was emotionally hurt when he returned. How was that so?"

"I cried enough tears for a lifetime during that time. All I wanted to do was find a reason to laugh again. Noah saved me from my own fate."

"Did he save you from your father? And why was your *datt* so upset when he came home?"

Mary closed her eyes and rested her forehead on her hand. "I couldn't tell him the truth. It would kill him for sure. So, I kept my secret from everyone except Noah. He was my only chance for any hope."

"What kind of secret would be so bad that it would have killed your father? You're talking in bits and pieces and I'm having trouble putting it all together."

Mary's low voice was barely audible. "Secrets ruin a family."

Mary looked at Rebecca and asked, "Did you hear what I said?"

"*Jah*, you said secrets ruin a family."

Silence filled the air and Rebecca waited for her to respond.

Mary turned her attention to the window and thought. *Lord, is it your will I take this secret to my grave? Will it really do any good if Andy and Eli know the truth?* She watched as a pair of mourning doves landed underneath the bird feeder, and the words she was dying to hear landed on her ears. *I am the truth, and the truth will set you free. Tell her Mary ...tell Rebecca the truth, it will set her free.*

Mary cleared her throat. "The truth will set you free."

"Excuse me?"

Mary smiled as Rebecca repeated. "The truth will set *me* free. Don't you mean the truth will set *you* free? Should I write that down?"

Mary reached for her quad stick and pointed to the bathroom. Rebecca laid the pen aside and helped Mary to the small room off the kitchen.

Rebecca held her elbow and asked, "Did whatever secret you kept from your father ruin your family?"

With an edge to her voice, Mary replied, "You don't see my son caring for me, do you? What do you think?"

Rebecca didn't know how to respond but wanted to be sure she remembered Mary's exact words when they returned to the table.

Instead of returning to the kitchen, Mary made Rebecca take her to the living room. Their time in Mary's story ended for yet another day, leaving her to ponder why she was so intent on telling her that the truth would set her free. Did Mary know more about her past than she gave the old woman credit for? Or had Eli confided things in his grandmother that should have been kept private?

Mary's soft snores matched the clock's pendulum, and Rebecca left her to nap and went outside. Carrying a glass of iced tea to the front porch, she lost herself in things of the past.

Laying her head on the back of the chair, she transported herself to the Farmers Market five years earlier. It was the start of her demise, and her jaw tightened as she remembered that hot June day.

Samuel had just delivered a load of strawberries to her father's furniture booth at the market, and she got bossy with him in an unladylike manner. When Anna pointed out her behavior, she became angry and left the booth in a fit of rage. How dare Anna embarrass her in front of the customers and in front of Samuel as well?

As the sights and sounds of the busy vegetable market played in her head, she tried to remember what Anna said to make her so mad. She remembered pushing a young mother aside as she blasted through a group of people and didn't look back when she heard the young woman scream.

Eli's heavy boots alerted her, and she opened her eyes when she felt him nearby.

Eli leaned on the porch railing. "Any more strange episodes with *Mommi* this morning?"

Rebecca stopped rocking the chair with her foot and looked up and thought. *Should I tell him what she said about secrets ruining a family.*

"*Nee*, but she did start to tell me about a secret that she was sure would upset her father had he found out."

"What secret is that?"

"I don't know. She had to pee, and then I lost her to a nap. She keeps saying bits and pieces but nothing that makes much sense."

Eli sighed. "May I make a suggestion?"

"Sure."

"Stop trying to make sense of it right now. Just let her talk."

"That's what I'm trying to do."

"Are you?"

"Okay, maybe I'm rushing her along too much. There is something she is trying to say, but she keeps beating around the bush about it."

"Maybe you're reading too much into it. Perhaps the message is more about something you are supposed to learn than letting some long-ago dark secret out."

His words hit a chord, and she nibbled on her bottom lip. Something in his eyes told her he was trying to tell her something. But just like his grandmother, he brushed by the true meaning with a riddle.

She picked up her glass and moved to the door. "I need to make dinner."

Eli continued to lean on the railing as he watched her move past him. Her gaze shifted back to him when he said, "Did I hit a nerve?"

"You tell me. Seems like you're trying to tell me something yourself."

Eli raised one eyebrow. "You're the one who has a few secrets in her past that might be prohibiting you from moving on. Ain't so?"

Rebecca snapped her head in his direction. "What's that supposed to mean?"

"Come on, Becca. We both know things didn't turn out between us like either of us hoped. When are you going to come clean with your part in it?"

He waited for her to respond, but she just looked at him with a perplexed frown. She closed the door behind her and leaned back on the door, thinking. *It's not that easy, Eli. I only did what I had to do to protect you from a fate worse than death. Nobody should have to suffer from my sins. Especially you.*

***

After Mary woke from her forenoon nap, Rebecca helped her to the kitchen. Then she proceeded to put dinner on the table.

Eli said few words during dinner and what he did say was directed at his grandmother. A heaviness hung in the air from their earlier conversation. A look of distress filled Mary's face when Eli asked her if he should make another appointment with the doctor.

"Heavens no. I'm in my eighties, and a little confusion comes with the territory."

Rebecca grinned at her statement, and Eli rolled his eyes and sighed. "I guess you got me there. But if Rebecca sees anything out of the normal, I'll be calling Dr. Smithson right away."

Mary tucked a tissue up under her sleeve. "You have better things to worry about than a senile old woman."

"And none are as important as you."

Rebecca changed the subject. "It's a lovely afternoon. How about we go sit in the garden, and we can get back to recording your story."

After Eli bowed his head for the second prayer, Rebecca took the chance to notice how his sandy blond hair was pushed tight against his temples. His jaw twitched as his lips moved silently. When he lifted his head, their eyes met, and she hoped he didn't notice she had failed to close her eyes at all.

Rebecca blushed. Something she didn't think she had ever done before. What was it about Eli that left her speechless? Rebecca felt Mary watching them. She dropped her head, gathered up his plate, and carried it to the sink. Oh, how she wished she could erase the past.

***

Rebecca followed Eli and Mary to the garden. She tucked the notebook and a lap quilt under her arm. After Eli had her situated on the bench, he glanced her way. "I'll be heading to the back pasture to fix a row of fence if you should need anything."

A flock of robins landed in the loose soil in the garden, digging for a worm or two. Both women stayed quiet as they watched the scene unfold.

Rebecca crossed her ankles and folded her hands on top of the notebook waiting for Mary to begin. In the silence, Rebecca started to remember how angry Eli had been when he caught Samuel and her together all those years ago. At the time, it was completely innocent. Still, she was sure it was precisely what Eli referred to in their earlier conversation. She didn't want to think about the past, but more importantly, she didn't want to talk about it, especially with Eli.

Mary's words rang in her head. *The truth will set you free.*

How could they? No one would understand and no one would care what haunted her so. She turned her attention back to Mary. As if the old woman knew exactly what was playing through her head, she said, "We all deserve to be happy."

Rebecca clenched her hands and studied Mary's face. She couldn't look into her eyes but for a moment before she had to turn away. Didn't she realize ...she *didn't* deserve to be happy?

Ignoring her comment, she opened the notebook. "Do you want to pick up where you left off? You just told me that secrets ruin a family. How so?"

"When *Datt* came back from the war, things were different. I was no longer his little girl. I had shamed him."

"How so? You were barely a young woman. How did you shame him?"

Lowering her head, Mary whispered, "I was with child."

A small gasp escaped Rebecca's lips, and she covered her mouth.

Mary continued, "There was no hiding my condition. Noah and I were sent to Willow Springs, where no one knew us."

"So is Eli's father, Andy, that child?"

"*Jah.*"

Rebecca wrote Mary's responses on the lined paper and waited patiently. She had so many questions, but she took Eli's advice and didn't rush her.

Mary brushed a drop from her nose with her sleeve. "Do you believe?"

"Do I believe what? In Jesus?" Rebecca creased her forehead. "*Jah.* Of course, I do. Do you?"

Mary waited for a few seconds then rubbed her temple.

"But do you really believe in Jesus?"

Mary's questions turned back to a riddle tale, and Rebecca tried to keep her frustration under control as she answered.

"I believe there is a Jesus." She paused and tapped the pen on the paper. "Do you want me to write these questions down?"

"If you need to." Mary pulled the lap quilt up with her good hand and tucked her limp arm under the quilted fabric.

"God doesn't want just a part of you now. He wants all of you, all the time."

Rebecca recorded Mary's words down and waited until Mary began again. "Things were different here in Willow Springs. No one knew Noah and me, and we could pretend we were a happily married couple. No one was the wiser."

"But I thought you said you were happy."

"As happy as you can be being married to a man who really didn't love you and only agreed to marry you to save face for his family."

"Mary? I'm so confused."

"It was just the beginning of a life full of lies and secrets. One lie turned into another, and before we knew it, we were living it like there was no way out."

"Did you ever go back to Lancaster?"

"*Nee*, and I never saw my father again. He died the same month Andy was born."

Rebecca noticed Mary started to tremble. "Are you cold? Do you need to go inside?"

"*Nee.* It's just sometimes the past is harder to face than the future."

Mary pointed to the paper. "Keep writing."

Mary turned her face to the sun and closed her eyes and repeated. "Secrets ruin a family."

Rebecca's tone took on an edge. "*Jah*, you said that a couple of times now."

Mary opened her eyes and glared at Rebecca. "But do you believe it? That one small secret cost me dearly, but I had kept my promise up until now."

"What promise was that?"

"That I would never share with Andy who his father was."

CHAPTER 11

M ary's house took on an eerie silence as Rebecca sprayed potato starch on Eli's Sunday shirt and ironed it. Lost in an array of confusing thoughts, she couldn't get past wondering why it was so important Mary kept Andy's father a secret. Eli's father had to be in his sixties, and she was dying to ask Eli if he knew what his grandmother was referring to.

What was it that Mary asked her? *Do you believe in Jesus?* That was a funny thing to ask her in mid-sentence. Of course, she believed in Jesus; she was baptized and all. It was all a mystery to her. The way Mary went back and forth from talking about Noah to asking her what and who she believed in. Not only was she confused, but she also felt Mary was getting more and more disoriented as the days went on. If she wanted to get to the bottom of Mary's story, she would need to keep her talking.

The screen door squeaked, and Rebecca let out a little yelp. "For heaven's sake, Eli, you startled me."

"How's *Mommi* this afternoon?"

"She's resting again. I'm afraid she hasn't been making much sense today. She goes from one subject to the next. In and out of thoughts with no order to any of them."

"Well, then I guess it's a good thing she has you to decipher things for her."

Eli didn't bother asking her any specific questions, and it was all she could do to keep what she'd been told to herself for the time being.

Eli popped a cookie in his mouth from the container on the counter before asking, "I need to run into town to get some more fencing supplies. Is there anything you need from Shetler's Grocery while I'm out?"

She moved to the refrigerator and rattled off a few items before turning to face him.

His eyebrows arched. "Would you like to go with me?"

Rebecca felt a surge in her cheeks. "I think I should stay around in case Mary wakes up."

He shrugged without saying a word, turned, and walked back out the door.

Was that a look of disappointment etched on his face? There she goes again. Not allowing herself to enjoy even the simplest of things. *What harm would it have done for her to ride along?*

***

Eli opted to take the open wagon and looked back toward the house one last time in hopes she changed her mind. Was he crazy to think she might let her guard down for even a few minutes to enjoy the spring day with him? *Mommi* would have been fine for the hour it would take them to get to town and back. Two steps ahead and one step back. Maybe he was chasing a dream, thinking she'd ever fess up and clear the air with him.

How would he ever get her to confide in him? There had to be more to the story than Samuel's confession. Perhaps another visit with Samuel would help him understand.

***

No matter the forlorn look on Eli's face, Rebecca knew she was doing exactly what she was meant to do. She couldn't help it; her father and Mary threw the two of them back together again. Nothing either of them could say or do would help correct the past. There was a rightness to keeping him at arm's length. She couldn't allow anything to get in her way of going forward with the life she planned out. Especially allowing herself to have a family of her own. She couldn't chance it. Not for one minute.

Turning her head toward Mary's room, she placed the iron back on the heat plate and followed the quiet whispers.

Mary was moving her head from side to side, mumbling. "Don't punish Noah."

Hoping to gain more insight into Mary's story, Rebecca waited and listened carefully.

Mary's voice rattled in a sleep-like state. "It's not fair. It's your fault ...you're the one who ..."

Not sure if she should wake Mary, she sat on the floor near the foot of the bed and listened.

As straightforward as the dust particles dancing in the ray of sunshine, Mary's following words flipped in her stomach to a point she covered her mouth. She pushed herself up from her knees and backed out of Mary's room, leaving the old woman to relive the pain in a dream. Rebecca's heart pounded in her ears. How long had Mary carried that horrible secret? And how could anyone as sweet as Mary Bricker be forced to live with such memories? And why did she feel the need to share such things now? For the life of her, she couldn't see how sharing any of it would make a difference now. *Oh*, she needed to talk to Eli. She had to tell him. Or did she?

Rebecca pulled her sweater around her tighter and sat in a rocker on the front porch, loathing a man she'd never met. Shock ran cold and deep inside Rebecca, and her heart ached for what Mary endured. She drew in a nose full of air and blew it out slowly. The peonies at the edge of the porch blew a sweet aroma by her, and it awoke her senses. She closed her eyes and tried to remember what Mary had shared with her about Noah.

Eli's grandfather didn't love Mary, but he sacrificed his life to give Mary and Andy the life they deserved. What kind of man did that? She knew Eli's character was cut from the same cloth without answering herself. He had done everything all those years ago to convince her to give them another shot. More than once, he told her he didn't care what she had done. He loved her and could forgive and forget anything as long as she would be honest with him. All he wanted was for her to be his wife.

At the time, she couldn't fathom any man forgiving a woman for such things. Her sins were unforgivable. But here again, a man much like Eli was willing to put genuine love aside to do the right thing. Noah had forgiven Mary, even though it wasn't Mary who needed forgiveness.

Moisture pooled in the corner of Rebecca's eyes, and she wiped it away while taking herself back to the screech of the truck tires and the cries of the young Amish woman at the market. It was the same dream she relived every day of her life. One of selfishness and ignorance at the cost of a woman and her child. If the woman at the market couldn't hold her child because of her carelessness, she would never allow herself any happiness either.

The scene played over in her head. *An argument with her schwester made her push her way through the crowd and separated the woman from her small child. When the woman's voice echoed off the open-air market, Rebecca ignored her cries and let the small toddler run in front of her and out into the parking lot.*

Rebecca's memory was engraved with the horrible sound. *The screeching tires and the thud of the toddler hitting the pavement a few feet away. Watching the commotion from the shadow of a delivery truck, she remembered Samuel looking up at her as he held the small child in his arms. His pleas to call 911 fell on deaf ears as she ran through the market.*

For days, Samuel pleaded with her to go to the bishop and confess what she had or hadn't done to save the young boy's life. After a month had gone by, Samuel felt responsible for his part. He succumbed to her blackmailing tactics to deceive Eli.

After so long, Rebecca reasoned away any role she played and used her life to sacrifice any meaningful happiness. Much like Noah did for Mary. But he held no fault for her secret.

The cooing of two doves forced Rebecca to open her eyes and follow the sound. She struggled against the resentment rising to overwhelming guilt that left a bad taste in her mouth. Why was God so intent on making her relive the woman's screams so often? Wasn't it enough that Emma and Samuel lost James, most likely as a pretense to her sin? When was enough, enough?

Lord help me. I don't want to be as old as Mary and still reliving the same old dream over and over again.

Following the doves, she marveled at how they gave no care in the world to her presence. They were perfectly content in picking up the leftover seeds the cardinals had pushed out of the bird feeder above.

She let out another breath and thought. *Is it too late for me? Much like it's probably too late for Eli and Andy. How will they ever understand? But it's not my secret to tell; it's Mary's.*

The air stood still as if someone stood in front of her to block the breeze, and she heard. *Rise up and step out of the darkness. The truth will set you free.*

Suddenly calm inside, Rebecca knew what she must do.

***

For a few moments, Mary opened her eyes and let the warmth of the sun land on her face. A strange buzzing in her ears pounded against her temples. A stab of pain warmed her ear and then settled over her forehead. The sensation forced her to bury her head deeper in her pillow, she called out.

"Noah."

Thoughts of her late husband filled her head, and an outstretched hand beckoned her forward. *Oh Lord, I've waited so long. Is it real?* Her weakened body lay beneath her as she floated toward the light. A voice was all around her, soothing her arrival. *Come, my daughter, look what I've prepared for you.*

Still, a part of her resisted. "But I need to explain things to Andy, and I haven't gotten through to Rebecca yet. She has so much to live for if she'll only let go."

He held His arms wide. *"You've set the seed; now trust me, my child. It's time."*

With a sigh of submission, Mary Bricker went home.

***

A sudden breeze blew through the wind chime at the end of the porch. Rebecca stood and watched the clapper bang against the tubes. Perhaps a short walk around the farm would clear her mind and help her find a way to set things right.

The quick thought of checking on Mary first floated away with the hollow sound at the end of the porch. Picking up her pace, she took the stairs two at a time and walked behind the barn to follow the fence line. New lambs abounded through the green fields without regard to anything but play.

Thinking of her carefree days as a child, she whispered, "Life had been so much easier then. To romp and play with no regard to what the future might bring. Oh, how I miss those days."

The afternoon sun cast shadows on the trees, and she stepped out in the sun to warm her shoulders. After turning the corner and stepping across a ditch, she moved to the side of the road just as she heard the dinner bell on the back of the porch clang repeatedly.

"What on earth?" she mumbled and took off, running toward the house.

Her heart sunk when she finally reached the back door. Eli stopped the bell and didn't say a word. The reason for the commotion was written all over his face.

"I was only gone for thirty minutes."

Eli sank to the steps and laid his face in his hands. Rebecca moved past him and ran to Mary's bed. There was a heaviness in the room, and Mary's distorted face took on a shade of gray.

Rebecca laid her fingertips on the side of Mary's wrist, even though she knew she'd feel no movement. When she stood, Eli was at her side. "I shouldn't have left her. I was only gone for a short time. I'm so sorry."

"You had no way of knowing."

Hadn't she? Once again, she put her selfish desires above her responsibilities.

"It's all my fault. God is punishing me, and you and Mary had to pay the price."

Rebecca turned to walk from the room, and Eli caught her arm. She stopped for a moment and looked into his eyes as she laid her hand on top of his. "I'll go get my father. He'll know what to do."

"Please don't go." Rebecca bit her lip. "I have to get someone."

"I'll go with you."

Rebecca moved his hand off her arm. "*Nee*, you stay."

The pleading in his sunken eyes did little to convince her otherwise. All she wanted to do was get as far away from Eli and his grandmother as she could. The dark cloud following her struck again. And no amount of assuring herself things weren't her fault did nothing to ease the pain behind Eli's blond lashes. The screen door slammed behind her.

***

Rebecca, Anna, and Emma helped clean Mary's house from top to bottom for the next two days while Eli, Samuel, and Daniel cleaned out the barn, making room for the furniture.

As Eli carried the last living room chair to the barn, making room for the rows of benches, a black sedan pulled into the driveway. An older version of Eli stepped out first, followed by who she assumed was Eli's mother. The older couple stood in the middle of the driveway and waited until the car pulled away before moving toward the porch. Rebecca watched Eli from across the yard and prayed he'd follow them to the house. When Eli called his father's name, the man stopped and changed his footing.

"*Datt?*"

"*Jah*, why are you so surprised?"

"I didn't think you'd make it in time."

"I'm not saying it was the ideal time to leave your *bruders* with all the planting, but out of respect for my mother, I came."

It didn't take much to notice Eli's jaw tighten at his father's response, even as far away as she was on the porch. His mother wrapped her arms around his middle and tenderly kissed Eli's cheek.

"It's good to see you, son."

"Thank you for coming. I do believe we have just about everything ready, and *Mommi's* body has been prepared, and her grave dug."

His father's voice, void of any emotion, replied, "Good I will need to head out tomorrow afternoon. Hopefully, you'll come to your senses and return to Lancaster with me."

Rebecca's hand began to cramp, and she loosened the hold she had on the bottle of window cleaner. For what seemed like an eternity, she held her breath, waiting for Eli to answer his father.

Eli hollered to her. "Becca, will you show my mother to my room?"

She set down the cleaner and rag, waved Eli's mother her way, and greeted her once she made it to her side.

"Becca Byler?"

"Rebecca."

The stout woman raised her chin and suppressed a slight smile in her direction. "Eli has spoken of you."

Without acknowledging the woman's probing, she led Mrs. Bricker to the back bedroom.

***

Eli turned on his heels. "I'm in no mood to discuss this with you now. As I have said a million times, I'm not moving back to Lancaster." Pushing his hands out before himself, he stated, "Besides, who will take care of all these sheep?"

His father stepped up his pace beside him. "I'm sure we could find some young farmer to take it over. It would be the perfect starter farm for any young family."

Eli stopped dead in his tracks. "Starter farm? I've poured more sweat and tears into this farm than any person I know. How could you think I would be ready to walk away from it all?"

The older man rolled his eyes. "It's a sheep farm! No son of mine should be tending sheep like a shepherd when he has a profitable dairy farm at his fingertips."

Pulling his father to the side of the barn and away from the group of men who gathered near the double barn doors, Eli stammered, "I can't believe we are having this conversation now. You haven't even paid your respect to your mother, and you're badgering me about leaving Willow Springs. For the final time, I'm not leaving this farm."

In a moment, he understood where his father stood, and his heart burst with what his father really thought of his *Mommi* Mary. "Couldn't you have thought of anyone but yourself for a minute?"

"I'm here, aren't I?"

"For face only. Had I known you'd be like this, I may not have called you until way after the funeral."

His father tipped his hat at the group of men heading their way and said, "You fail to forget this farm is mine, and I've only let you play farmer until the time came when I could take back what was rightfully mine."

Eli let out a slight groan and sucked in a deep breath as his father whispered, "Playtime is over."

Eli fought to move his feet but couldn't take his eyes off the man who walked across the yard. Had he been so blind all these years to see his father cared about no one but himself? How could a woman as sweet as his grandmother raise a child who was so outright evil? He swore right there and then that there wasn't an ounce of Andy Bricker he wanted to claim as his own.

CHAPTER 12

Rain pounded against the windowpane as Rebecca tried to concentrate on her father's words. As one of the newest ministers, he delivered Mary's funeral service. Eli's tiny home was bursting with one hundred or more neighbors and friends who came to pay their final respect.

Anna sat to her left and tapped her knee when she leaned on the cool glass. Even having her *schwester* close wouldn't stop the urge to run home and far away from prying eyes. While they didn't say it, she was sure each one was blaming her for Mary's death. She had been hired as her nursemaid, and she wasn't there when the old woman took her last breath.

Even Eli's typically soft and endearing eyes were cold and lifeless when he looked her way. For a fleeting moment, two days ago, Rebecca was sure she knew what she needed to do to move her life forward. God proved she wasn't worth His forgiveness. Once again, she was responsible for another person's death. It was time she left Willow Springs for good. The further she was away from those she cared about, the less likely God would take vengeance on those she loved. Rebecca twisted the tissue in her hands and closed her eyes.

First, it was the toddler at the market. I didn't stop him from running through the crowd when I could have. Next, it was Mamm. She died on my watch. If I hadn't gone outside to brush the straw out of the alpacas, I would have been there to ease her last breaths. Then Emma's James. And now, Mary. How could I be so selfish as to not be by her side when she needed me the most?

The doctor said nothing could have stopped another stroke from taking her life. But I don't believe it. I should have been there. If not for her, then for Eli.

Anna reached down and squeezed Rebecca's hand when she failed to stand. It was their turn to file past Mary's body. As the row in front of them emptied, Rebecca noticed Eli's mother wiping a tear from her cheek.

Frowning slightly, Rebecca chastised the woman in her head. What did Eli's mother know about Mary? Did she really have the right to mourn? Something dark was working beneath the surface. The change that had been taking place in Rebecca's heart since coming to care for Mary hardened with one look at Eli's parents.

Rage raced up the back of her neck, and it was all she could do to keep the words from spilling off her tongue. If it hadn't been for Anna's warm hand in hers, she might have marched right up to the woman. Regardless of the backlash she would have gotten from her father and the bishop.

Anna leaned in close. "What is it? You're trembling."

Rebecca pulled her hand away and nudged her *schwester* to move forward. "It's nothing. I just need some air."

Rebecca fell into step in line, filing past Mary's body, and looked around the room until she laid eyes on Eli. His head was dropped, and his hands were folded in his lap. The starched white shirt she had just ironed the other day looked stiff and unnatural on his slumped shoulders. His father sat to his left with his head held high.

Taking in a deep breath and letting it out again, she felt Eli's anguish. There was no doubt he loved his grandmother and would miss her terribly. It was evident to anyone who knew them that Mary was more a mother to Eli than his own. Well, it was at least obvious to her. The room started to close in around her, and it was all she could do to make it to the porch. The rain had slowed, and only a few sprinkles were left in the air. The harmonious dark cloud had moved to the east, and tiny slivers of blue could be seen edging their way among the budding trees.

It would still be an hour before Mary's body moved to a pine box and taken to the Willow Springs cemetery only a mile away. Too many times over the last five years had she walked past the field lined with small white grave markers a short distance away.

Stepping off the porch, Rebecca moved to the side of the house and past the kitchen garden. Peeking up through a mound of dirt was a cluster of the same Johnny Jump-ups she had destroyed just a week ago. The small yellow and purple petals lifted their faces toward the sky and greeted her with a smile as she knelt to run her fingers over the velvety petals.

A warmth penetrated her fingers, and Mary's voice echoed in her ears. *Secrets are simply part of our life stories that have been forced into hiding. Secrets ruined my family, don't let it ruin yours.*

A sob settled into the back of Rebecca's throat, and she got her foot caught in the hem of her black dress when she tried to stand.

A strong hand cupped her elbow. "I'd hate for your good clothes to be caked with mud from a fall into *Mommi's* garden."

She saw the muscles in his face tense slightly after he spoke. She stayed quiet as he swallowed hard and moved to the side, so she could get her footing.

"*Mommi* loved this place. I should have done more to keep it up for her."

Eli Bricker had the tenderest heart of anyone she knew. Much too sweet for the likes of her. "She understood, I'm sure of it. You had your hands full with running the farm."

She was sorry she said anything when his jaw clenched again, and he looked off in the direction of the barn. "It's not my farm; it's my father's."

A new wave of tightness filled her chest. "What do you mean, your father's? You made this land what it is today. Your father didn't."

He didn't answer but looked toward the row of buggies starting to form a line down Mystic Mill Road. "I suppose it's time."

She stood still and watched him walk to the barn. The blond curls at the nape of his neck wrapped up to the rim of his black felt hat, and it was there she said her goodbyes. Both to Mary and to Eli.

***

Spring turned into early summer as Rebecca resumed her duties at *Stitch 'n Time*. On the other hand, Anna fell back into step with staying behind the curtain while Rebecca handled the customers. Even walking past Eli's house left Rebecca in a state of disarray, so it was better she pushed any thoughts of him far away.

The bell above the door chimed, and Rebecca looked up from her seat at the counter. Her eyes widened when Eli's broad shoulders encased the doorway.

He moved his attention to Anna, who sat at the spinning wheel and back to her. "May I have a word with you?"

She bit her bottom lip and waited for him to continue. She hadn't laid eyes on him in almost four weeks and went out of her way to stay clear of any chance of running into him. Her mind was still swarming with a way to leave Willow Springs, but a plan hadn't presented itself yet.

He pushed the door back open. "Can we step out on the porch?"

She glanced over her shoulder toward Anna and shrugged before heading to the door.

Eli held the door open until she passed through. Once the door closed, he took off his hat and twirled it in his fingers. He moved to the edge of the stairs and stared off toward her father's house.

"It's out of my hands."

The tone of his voice was unlike anything she had ever heard. The pain in his words spoke so much, even without her knowing what he was referring to. She never realized a person could communicate a feeling in so few words.

She walked to his side and looked at him bleakly. "What's out of your hands?"

"*Mommi* Mary left the farm and all of its acreage to me with a stipulation."

Rebecca folded her hands, brought them to her chin, and sighed. "That's good news, *jah*?"

"Depends."

"Depends on what?"

"It depends on the person she left it to. And she'll need to agree to something that she has no desire for. It's the only way to keep the farm away from my father."

There was no doubt he was referring to her the way he said *she*. Rebecca felt a heaviness in the pit of her stomach, and she was afraid to ask. "*Me?*"

Eli sat on the top step and motioned his head for her to sit beside him. "You'd better sit, or you may fall once I explain."

Rebecca scooped her dress behind her knees and sat on the wooden step. "You're starting to worry me. What is it, and how can I help you keep the farm?"

Eli secured his hat on his knee and rested his forearms on his thighs. "Seems *Mommi* Mary had this planned for a long time. Even before she had her first stroke. About this time last year by the looks of it."

With an edge of impatience Rebecca asked, "Had what planned?"

"To sign the farm over to me."

"But that's good news. It won't go to your father like he threatened. How can that be a bad thing? You won't be forced to go back to Lancaster."

Eli looked straight ahead. "Lancaster was never an option."

He drew a shaky breath and let it out slowly. "The farm comes with a clause. And that clause is you."

She pressed her hand to her temple. "Eli, you're making no sense."

"The only way I can keep the farm is if I marry you. The farm, house, and land will become mine the day I marry. And then it will become ours."

Breath escaped Rebecca's lips, and she shook her head from side to side. "What?"

Eli reached into his back pocket and pulled two letters from his trousers. "She explains it in these. She left a letter for both of us. I found them in her room last week when I was searching for any paperwork for the house."

She took the white envelope from his hands with her name clearly printed across the front.

"I didn't open yours, but I'm sure it's similar to mine."

"And if I don't agree?"

"The farm and the land go back to my father."

"Why? I don't understand. Why would your grandmother do such a thing?"

Eli stood. "I'm sure she explains everything in your letter. I didn't come here to beg you to marry me. Especially since I know it's the last thing you want to do. But I had to tell you what I'm up against."

Rebecca looked at him, eyes troubled. "I don't even know what to say."

"Don't say anything right now. Read the letter. You know where to find me when you want to talk."

The white envelope had a cluster of pansies faded into the background and smelled like Mary's almond cherry hand lotion. When she brought it to her nose, she was transported back into Mary's room, and her soothing voice played in her head.

A songbird cooed overhead as Eli backed his buggy away from the shop and clicked his tongue to get the horse to pick up its pace. The clip-clop of its hooves kept time to the wagon wheels as it pulled out onto Mystic Mill Road. The hardened blacktop set the steady beat of the horse's metal shoes in motion. As it faded, all that could be heard was the bird perched on the maple tree beside the porch.

Rebecca was afraid to slide her fingers along the seal and reveal her future. The loneliness she had felt over the last five years of keeping everyone at bay tried to escape. She desperately wanted to keep her true identity hidden far away from anyone it might hurt. How could Mary do such a thing? She could hardly breathe as she slipped her fingers under the flap. The riddles Mary kept twisting around their conversations played in her head like the television she'd seen at The Sandwich Shoppe in downtown Willow Springs. Repeating itself repeatedly until the same message was embedded in your brain.

The white-lined paper had deep creases like they were ironed in to make a point. When she unfolded it, Mary's perfect penmanship pulled her in.

Rebecca,

As this may come as a shock to you, please know my decision concerning my grandson didn't come lightly. I may be an old woman and one who should keep her nose out of the affairs of my grandson, but when it comes to knowing what is best for him, I do.

You may think you've kept yourself hidden beneath layers of lies and secrets, but you're only fooling yourself.

I've watched you throw away your life, and I refuse to let this one last chance I have to save it pass me by.

If you're reading this letter, I assume I could not help you and Eli see you were meant for each other while I was alive. If that is the case, I have set a plan to force you two to realize there is more to life than what you're both running from.

There is no hiding from me, as there is no way to hide from God. I was there, and I saw it all. I watched from afar as you faded into the shadows filled with shame and guilt. Quit hiding Rebecca; it's time to face the truth. It's time to call on Jesus and ask for forgiveness. His truth will set you free.

I've spent my life running from the truth, and it cost me my son. Don't make the same mistakes. My God is your God, and he has a forgiving heart. He sent his son to die for our sins, which means yours too.

I may not be the best with words, and I can only speak of my own experiences, but I've learned in my long life that if God has placed me near a dry well, it's for a reason. At every turn, He's preparing me for something bigger. A new spiritual place beside Him. In those dark and dreadful times when I felt the furthest from Him, isolated and alone, I heard Him the loudest.

Find yourself, Rebecca, step out of the shadows. Let God direct you, even push you if need be, to a place where you feel His presence in your life. It's only there that you will find the peace you are chasing.

Now onto the purpose of this letter…

Andy will do everything in his power to take this farm away from Eli, and I'm bound to stop that from happening. I refuse to make excuses for my son's actions, and he will face his maker one day, the same as me.

Eli's great-grandfather bought us this farm, and it came with a similar stipulation. The only way Noah could get a farm of his own was to agree to marry me in the process. At the time, it was a great burden for him to leave the woman he loved to save me from a tarnished reputation. But Noah had the heart of a saint, and he sacrificed himself to protect me. I've always felt this house was blessed by the Lord because Noah put his wants and desires aside to do His work.

I see Noah in Eli. I know this is so much to ask. But step out in faith and give Eli a chance to show you a life you so deserve.

Remember, Rebecca, you are only fooling yourself. God sees your heart, and it's His job to restore it if you let Him.

Often God will not allow us to continue in a place that seems safe and secure. But shows us a path that takes us places that leaves us uncomfortable and vulnerable. This is the place God has put on my heart to show you. He wants your faith primed, ready to be His ambassador when you are called into service. He'll often call us to a place in waiting to prepare us for bigger things.

This is my blessing to you, Rebecca. Take this house beside Eli and make it a home. Love will follow, I promise.

Mary

A nagging fear coursed through her. She could hear her inner bell chime a warning to run away. Rebecca shivered inside. *I can't do it. Eli will suffer just like Mary did. It worked out for Mary, but it won't for me. A dark cloud will follow us, I'm sure of it.*

This was too much to ask. Regardless of whether Eli would lose the farm or not, how could he agree to marry her? He didn't even love her. She was shocked he would even consider it. Rebecca flipped the letter over and found Mary's words. *Eli's great-grandfather bought us this little farm, and it came with a similar stipulation.*

Defensive anger welled up inside of her, and she mumbled, "He bought you a farm to keep your mouth shut, and you let him! How could you, after what he did to you?"

A torrent of angry words spilled from her mouth as she tried to wrap her head around what Mary was asking her to do. And Eli, how could he even consider it? She rubbed the back of her neck with her free hand and shoved the letter in her apron pocket with the other. Letting a long breath escape her lips, she whispered. *"If you see my hear,t Lord, then you can see this is plain crazy. I'd just as soon stay alone than agree to a loveless marriage. It might have worked for Noah and Mary, but there is no way it would work for Eli and me."*

She stood, placed her hands on her hips, and stretched her back out just as Mary's voice rang in her ears. *The truth will set you free.*

In a disgusted tone, she yelped, Ugh!

CHAPTER 13

Wilma's voice etched a piercing tone as Rebecca's name rang across the yard.

"What?"

"Your father wants a word with you."

Tucking Mary's letter down deep in her pocket, she stepped off the porch and tried to swallow down her frustration. The last thing she needed was a lecture, and she murmured her complaint on the way to the house. "What have I done now?"

The squeak of the screen door announced her arrival, and her father called to her from the kitchen. "In here."

"Wilma said you wanted to talk to me."

Wilma sat to his left and had her hands wrapped around a mug. Her father pushed away his glass of tea and sat back in his chair. The way he took in a breath and puffed out his chest told Rebecca that she wouldn't like what he had to say.

"I see Anna isn't helping the customers anymore since you returned to the shop."

Rebecca took a seat at the table. "She's more comfortable behind the curtain."

"In whose opinion? Yours or hers?"

"I suppose hers, but I didn't ask. We just took back our original places once I was done working at Mary's."

Her father leaned his elbows on the arm of the chair and laced his fingers together. "That's a problem."

"Why so?"

"We were noticing Anna was starting to come out of her shell while you were away. Now that you're back, she's reverting to her old ways."

Rebecca crossed her legs and folded her arms across her chest. "Anna's always been a bit timid around people. Why is that an issue?"

Wilma was quick to add. "Because she hides behind you, and that's not healthy."

Raising her head in the woman's direction, she answered, "So you think that I purposely hinder my own *schwester*? And stop looking at me that way!"

Jacob cleared his throat. "We're only trying to say that Anna was doing so well in your absence."

Rebecca's shoulders hunched slightly. "And you feel I'm holding her back?"

Her father picked up his glass and took a long drink before answering. "*Jah*."

Wilma pushed a letter across the table in her direction. "My family in Willow Brook needs help at their farm stand this summer, and we think it best you leave Willow Springs for a short time."

"*Datt*?"

"Now get that look off your face. It's only for a short time, and it will give Anna the time she needs to step out on her own. She can't hide behind you her whole life."

Rebecca stopped and stared. She couldn't believe what they were suggesting. *Stitch 'n Time* was her idea, and now they wanted her to walk away from her business to work a farm stand twenty miles away.

Wilma pushed the letter closer. "My *schwester* says you can stay with her for the summer. They have a lovely farm at the edge of town, and it's only a short thirty-minute walk to the market."

"No way!" Her eyes were hot.

The frown on her father's face and the way he straightened his shoulders told her more than words could express.

A coldness seeped into the room and sent a chill up her arms. "You can't be serious."

"Look, we didn't come to this decision easily. We could have just as quickly sent Anna away, but you are the stronger of the two. We are afraid your *schwester* wouldn't fare well away from home."

"I can't believe it. You're really suggesting I move away from Willow Springs?" Rebecca sprang up and paced the kitchen. "This is my life, not yours."

Shame gripped her. Not that she hadn't tried to figure out how to leave Willow Springs herself, but being forced to leave? That was like she was being backed into a corner with no way out.

Wilma pulled the letter back into her possession and folded it neatly on the table. "For heaven's sake, Rebecca, you're being over dramatic. It's only for the summer. It's not like we're sending you off forever."

"The summer? That's when we are the busiest with preparing fiber for the rest of the year. The shop slows down in the summer, and it gives us time to clean and spin enough yarn to get us through the winter. Besides, I've already agreed to buy more wool from Eli. Anna could never take care of that all on her own."

Her father pushed his chair out and stood. "Then Anna can hire someone to help her."

Rebecca stopped in her tracks and faced her father. "I can't go to Willow Brook."

He turned and looked her straight in the eye. "Give me one good reason why."

Without thinking about what she was about to say, she blurted out. "Eli asked me to marry him."

Wilma let out a gasp. "Thank the Lord."

Her father's lip turned upward. "And when was he going to speak to me about this?"

Rebecca dropped her head. "I suppose after I gave him my answer."

Jacob grabbed his straw hat off the table and headed to the door. "I guess this changes a good many things."

Wilma seemed to be enjoying herself, and the smirk on her face moved to a solemn look. "Oh my, we have so much to do."

Rebecca hadn't given one thought to the plans she just put in motion. In the span of just two weeks and after the bishop published them at church the next day, she would be Mrs. Eli Bricker. Sitting back down in her chair, she rested her hands on the table and covered her eyes with the palm of her hands. *What had she done?*

Wilma moved to the drawer at the end of the counter and pulled out a pad of paper and ink pen.

"A dress, we need to go buy fabric. And you'll need a new white apron. You'll want royal blue for your wedding dress, right? And the meal. I'll need to meet with the neighbors and see who can help make pies. Oh, and the cleaning. This farm hasn't been cleaned from top to bottom in a good long time. The invitations. You and Anna will need to get started on them right away. You and Eli will need to begin hand-delivering them on Monday. Do you think his parents will come from Lancaster?"

Rebecca flipped her head back and blew out a long breath from her lips in an unladylike manner. "Stop! I can't talk about this right now."

Wilma squared her shoulders. "But we must. We only have two weeks before the wedding. There is so much to do. But first, I'll need to write my *schwester* and tell her you won't be coming to help at the market."

Rebecca stood and moved to the sink. She ran a cool glass of water and downed it all before walking back outside. Something inside her ruptured, leaving a wave of sorrow in its path. She had just agreed to marry Eli, knowing full and well he didn't love her. Mary's plan was put in motion, and there was nothing she could do now but accept her fate.

***

Eli walked home, knowing Rebecca had most likely read *Mommi's* letter. Once he reached the barn, he sat on a bale of straw and pulled his grandmother's letter from his pocket. He still couldn't believe Rebecca held his future in her hands. Would she realize what it would cost her for him to stay in Willow Springs? Or better yet, would she even care?

My Dearest Eli,

My heart aches to know you most likely are dealing with an array of emotions right now. You are so much like my Noah. He wore his heart on his sleeve, much like you do. I can't thank you enough for coming to care for me all these years. I most likely would have perished long ago from loneliness had you not come along. You were an answer to my prayers.

There are so many things I had hoped to explain to you before I left, but if you are reading this letter, I didn't get that chance. First, I want to say how sorry I am that you had to be in the middle of your father's and my problems. Please don't hold any ill feelings for your father. Andy is a good man; he just had the influence of your Great-Grandfather Bricker longer than he did Noah.

Eli stopped and read the line over again. Why wouldn't *Mommi* refer to Noah as my grandfather? So many things I don't understand. He shook his head and continued reading.

I know for sure your heart is on the right path. We have studied the bible together, and I'm confident you are a follower of Jesus. So many of the young people here in Willow Springs are not taught the truth in Jesus. They're still following our past

212

ways of works over faith. Our leaders don't know any better, and I pray someday that will change. I believe it will come about with your help. I'm not sure how I know that, but I think it will happen in your lifetime. Please continue to study your English bible and break the cycle starting with your family. Teach them the truth from the beginning, and that begins with Rebecca.

By now, you have found the deed to this house and farm. You will see that I have left it both to you and Rebecca. If you are reading this letter, I failed at getting you past the things that kept you apart. You can't hide your feelings from me. I saw it on your face every time you looked her way. Just as Rebecca hasn't been able to hide them either. I know what has caused her great pain, and it's your place to get to the bottom of it. The woman loves you and always has. She just can't see it through years of lies and secrets. If anyone is going to pull her from the depths of her despair, it's Jesus and you.

Please forgive me for putting you in a position of having to force Rebecca's hand in marriage. I'm not sure if she will accept your proposal, but I know she has the heart to do the right thing. And if she can't see that, God will continue to work on restoring the spirit He gave her. Please see past her hard exterior and know all she has done was to save you from what she thinks she is protecting you from.

I had hoped that I could have helped her see the path God wanted her to walk on by the time I passed. But again, if you are reading this letter, I failed, and now it's up to you.

She will balk at an arranged marriage, but it's the only way I could convince your father to allow you to stay in Willow Springs and on this farm. He agreed to my wishes, only if you were married. As you can see in the agreement, the farm reverts to Andy if you are not married within three months of my passing.

Eli, please know that not all marriages start out with love. Often our plans are not what God intended. But it's our job to lay our lives at his feet and accept whatever season he puts us in.

God has put you in a position of great sacrifice. You may think you have no other option than to concede to your father's wishes. But please, Eli, don't think of it as a great burden but as a great gift. Rebecca needs a man of God to lead her, and God chose you. Why else do you think no other woman has crossed your path in the last five years? God knows how to work through the most challenging circumstances to better his kingdom.

I promised to take the most disturbing secret to my grave, and it cost me my family. Please don't let Rebecca succumb to the same fate. Show her that she deserves to be loved, first by her heavenly father and then by you.

All my love,

Mommi Mary

The clip-clop of an approaching buggy pulled his attention away from the letter, and he slipped it in his back pocket as he walked to the opened barn door.

Jacob Byler pulled his buggy to a stop at Eli's feet, and Eli led the horse to the hitching post. Jacob stepped down from the buggy and wrapped the reins around the iron stake.

Silence reigned for several seconds as both men found their footing. Jacob removed his hat and motioned toward the house. "May I have a few moments with you?"

"Of course." Eli raised his hand and let the older gentleman step before him.

Once inside, Eli pointed toward the table. "Can I offer you something to drink?"

"No, I won't be long. What I have to say will only take a few minutes."

Eli felt his legs buckle under his weight and chose to sit to hear Jacob out. By the look on the man's face, he wasn't sure he'd like what he had to say.

"Rebecca tells me you asked her to marry you?"

Eli jerked his head in Rebecca's father's direction. "In a roundabout way, I did. But she has not given me her answer yet."

Jacob took a seat at the table. "I'm certain she will. If not, she will be leaving for Willow Brook in the morning."

"Willow Brook? For what?"

"*Jah*. To work."

Fear gripped Eli for a split-second. "I'm confident she'll choose to stay."

Jacob laid his hat on the table. "The girl is troubled. You know that, *jah*?"

Eli could hardly believe his ears. Had Rebecca's father come to tell him to stay clear of his daughter by pointing out her flaws?

"Excuse me?"

"The girl has some issues, and I want to be sure you are aware of her shortcomings long before you are stuck with her for life."

Eli leaned back in his chair and tried to understand why Jacob would speak so ill of his own daughter. "I'm fully aware of Rebecca's shortcomings. But to be quite honest, I'm bothered you felt the need to come and point them out to me. Could it be that you're part of the problem?"

"Son, I didn't come here to talk you out of marrying her or get in a disagreement with you. I just want to be sure you are fully aware of what you are taking on when it comes to Rebecca."

Eli smiled wryly. "How about you tell me then?"

Jacob crossed his hands over his chest. "To begin, her tongue gets her in trouble most days."

"Nothing I can't handle."

"Next, she has a prideful nature and steps out of line more often than not."

Eli smirked. "I quite like to be challenged on occasion."

"Lastly, she'd much rather be in the barn than in the kitchen. Won't get many good meals out of that one."

Eli tapped his thumbs on the arm of his chair. "I didn't starve when she was here taking care of my grandmother. I didn't find her meals displeasing."

Jacob stood and put his hat back on. "I guess you know what you're getting into then. I assume you'll give the bishop a date before tomorrow so you can be published properly?"

"As soon as I know, you'll know too."

For the first time in his life, he felt like a man. Standing up to Rebecca's father had felt good. Maybe *Mommi* Mary was on to something. Perhaps it was his job to save the girl, and it didn't hurt that he genuinely cared for her. Just listening to her father talk wrongly about her left a sour taste in his mouth. He didn't see Jacob out but stayed planted in his chair until a soft knock pulled his attention to the front door.

***

Rebecca ducked around her father's buggy and quietly walked around the backside of the house, hoping to eavesdrop on her father and Eli's conversation. Had she known her father was heading to Eli's, she would have stayed clear until he returned. But now that she was here, her curiosity got the better of her.

The warm spring day meant Eli had the windows opened to let a fresh breeze air out the house. It would be easy for her to stoop under the kitchen window to hear what her father had come to say.

Hearing how her father talked about her behind her back made her sink to the ground. Yes, he said nothing she didn't already know, but to hear her own father speak so unkindly of her tore at her soul. She went numb from the top of her head to the soles of her shoes.

Out of pure embarrassment, she let tears fall to her chin and thought. *Oh Datt, how could you? Eli already knows all those things, but did you have to point them out so harshly?*

After hearing Eli defend her, she knew what she needed to do. If she couldn't trust her own father's love to come to her defense, how could she expect God or even Eli to forgive her for her past mistakes?

She waited for her father's buggy to pull away before she left her hiding spot and headed to the front door. She pushed a few loose strands of her chestnut hair back under her *kapp*, softly tapped on the door, and waited.

The scrape of Eli's chair across the linoleum sent shivers up her arms. In a swift moment, she closed her eyes and prayed. *Lord, please help me do right by Eli.*

CHAPTER 14

Eli looked over Rebecca's shoulder as he opened the door. How long had she been standing there, and had she heard the conversation he had with her father? Every window in the house was open, and it wouldn't have been hard to overhear. He noticed she held his grandmother's letter in her hand.

Glancing down at the paper she gripped between her fingers, he asked, "Are you okay?"

"*Nee.*"

He tipped his chin, his eyes tender. "Would you like to come in?"

Rebecca ducked past him and waited until he guided her to the pair of rockers in the front room. "Your father was just here."

"*Jah*, I saw."

"You told him I asked you to marry me?"

"*Jah*."

He raked his fingers through his hair, and his tone was flat. "It would have been nice if you had told me first."

Her eyes grew moist as she lowered herself to the chair. "I've made a terrible mistake by blurting that out before I gave it much thought. I had just read Mary's letter, and then *Datt* and Wilma told me they were sending me off to Willow Brook for the summer."

Eli took a seat in the adjoining chair and rested his elbows on his knees. "So your answer?"

The tears fell harder. "Eli, I just don't know. I thought I could live with what Mary was asking me to do, but listening to my *datt* just now, why would you want me?"

Leaning forward, he clasped his hands between his knees. "I was afraid you might have heard us."

Rebecca wiped a tear from her chin and stared out the window. "Why did you leave Lancaster?"

He propped his elbows back on his knees and rested his chin in his hands. "I knew if I stayed one day longer, I would give into my father's dream and not wait on what God had planned for me."

He unfolded himself from the chair and moved to the window. "I suppose to my family, I made the biggest mistake of my life."

Rebecca set the chair in motion. "And if you went back now?"

Without an ounce of hesitation, he replied, "I'd be miserable. God called me to Willow Springs for a purpose."

"A purpose?"

His brows rose. "*Jah*, I'm just not sure what it is yet."

She looked at him in defeat. "I'm certain your purpose wasn't to get tangled up with the likes of me."

He grinned wickedly. "I'd do it all over again if it meant we would cross paths again."

"How can you say such things after my father just pointed out all of my shortcomings?"

"I don't need your father telling me anything. I know all there is to know about Becca Byler."

She darted out of her chair and headed to the door. "You're wrong. You only know a few surface things. You don't know anything about the real Rebecca Byler." She found the doorknob and struggled to get it opened.

He rushed to her side and grabbed her arm to turn her around. When she stumbled, she fell against the wall, and he towered over her with his arm holding himself up above her head. "How about you tell me then?"

She tried to duck under his arm, but he put his leg out to stop her and pulled her back into his hold. She leaned back on the wall and moved her head to the side, so he couldn't see her eyes.

With a gentle nudge, he pulled her chin forward. She ducked out of his grip. He pulled her chin back to the center and said, "Tell me all the things you've kept hidden in that pretty little head of yours. I want to hear it all. Nothing you say will shock me or change how I feel."

She cringed at his last statement and sucked in a deep breath chastising herself again.

"Isn't it enough my own father can see all my faults? Why would I need to point them out again to you?"

He cupped her face tenderly. "Because I don't care what your father thinks." He took his finger and tapped her chest. "I know what's in here."

She tried to twist from his hold. "You know no such thing."

Eli dropped his hands and wrapped his fingers around her wrists. A flash of red moved from her neck to her cheeks and settled on her lips. Her heart took a leap as he leaned in closer.

"What are you afraid of?"

Her green-flecked eyes took on a panicked shade. "That God will punish you for my past mistakes."

"Our God isn't like that. He is forgiving and loving."

"Your God, but not mine."

He pulled her hands to his chin and took a few moments before he answered.

"You have so much to learn. Won't you please let me help you be set free from whatever you think you've done that is so bad God would punish you?"

She moved her head to the side and whispered, "It would be so easy for me to give in and think we could go on like I didn't have a past. But I can't do it."

He stopped her and tipped her chin back so their eyes met. "No, you can't, but together we can with God's help."

Rebecca pushed him aside and reached for the door. Her throat tightened when he replied, "I'm only asking one more time. Tell me what is so horrible you'd throw your whole life away because of it."

Tension filled the air for a few seconds; then, she slid down the wall and rested her head on her folded knees.

Eli fell to one knee and rested his hand on her shoulder. "It's time. This has gone on long enough."

Her face showed signs of complete and utter defeat. The rims of her eyes were red, and her face turned a ghastly white. With the back of her sleeve, she wiped the moisture from her face. "You talk about how God is loving and forgiving. But my own father can't accept me for who and what I am. How do you expect me to believe my heavenly father will forgive me?"

Eli moved to the wall beside her, leaned back, and rested his elbows on his propped-up knees. "You know we have more in common than you think we do."

"How so?"

"Our earthly fathers could use some work."

Rebecca nodded solemnly and gave a slight snicker. "I suppose so. But not as much as me."

Eli stretched out his legs, and Rebecca followed suit. "Our fathers really don't know any better. They only do what their fathers before them had done. They follow a bunch of man-made traditions and rules and don't know the true meaning of following Jesus. If you read the Old Testament, God got angry more than once when His people used idols in place of Him. In my books that's exactly what this long list of rules is to me. Nothing but a bunch of false idols."

"Eli? How can you say such things?"

"Because it's the truth. Do you know what a truth seeker is?"

Rebecca thought for a moment and answered, "*Nee,* I don't think I've ever heard that term before."

"It means we seek to discover the truth as it is clearly written in the bible."

"What does that have to do with our fathers?"

"Our fathers come from a generation where rules and traditions mean more than trusting in Jesus as our one and only way to heaven."

"Eli, you're confusing me. The things you speak of will get you excommunicated in a minute. You have to know that."

"Oh, believe me, I do. Half of the reason it's so important I stay in Willow Springs. But I can't do that without your help."

Rebecca pushed herself up to her feet. "Oh no! I have enough problems right now; I don't need to worry about being shunned. The last thing you need is my help with anything."

Eli rolled to his side and flipped his long legs underneath him until he stood beside her. He took her arms in his hands.

"Look, God's plans are rarely meant to heal every pain. His intention is to heal our hearts first by teaching us something, to show us things about ourselves, and to take our human desires away and replace them with His will."

Eli wrapped his fingers around her hands and brought them back up under his chin. "Becca, we are all a work in progress. God takes every one of our fears and insecurities away, so we can be more useful for His future purposes."

He took his finger and tapped her heart. "You are meant to be His ambassador, just like I am, and you can't be that until you seek his forgiveness."

A new set of tears toppled over her dark lashes. "But you don't understand. My own father thinks I'm not worthy enough. How will God ever forgive me for all I've done, let alone you saddle yourself with the likes of me for a lifetime?"

Eli kissed her fingertips. "His provision will only come when you submit yourself to him."

Rebecca closed her eyes against the sudden tears. She wished she had never come. She wished she had never heard what her father honestly thought of her. And most of all, she wished she hadn't let Eli get so close. It only made it harder to tell him no.

"I'm sorry, Eli, it's too much. God will never forgive me, and I cannot let you carry the weight of my burden." She twisted from his grip. And this time, he let her go.

***

The door bounced when she let it go behind her. She didn't dare turn around and look back. The sight of Eli in the doorway would have killed her. He'd fought hard. She'd give him that. But he had no idea what harm would come to him and his family if he brought her into it.

Her feet bounced against the pavement, and her heart took on a new beat. It was like she was running for her life. Far away from Willow Springs with no plans of returning. Her father's plan to send her to Willow Brook was precisely what she needed. Little did he know it was the perfect plan.

Once she made it down Eli's hill, she slowed her pace and stopped to catch her breath. She let her mind drift back to Eli's words. *His intention is to heal our hearts first by teaching us something.* She brushed a hair away that escaped her *kapp* and mumbled, "How on earth am I supposed to learn a thing from all of this? I've learned enough over the years, and that is to keep everyone I care about at arm's length. And besides, haven't I learned enough already. Especially that my own father, couldn't care less about me."

A warm breeze tickled her nose, and she stopped to watch a pair of new lambs romp through the field at the edge of Eli's pasture. A memory as vivid as the day it happened came to mind.

Anguish filled her until she thought her knees would buckle at the weight. It was the day her mother died. The air stood still, and the cries of her *schwesters* echoed off her mother's bedroom walls. The day she realized it was her fault that God took their mother away. Because of her sins, *Mamm* was gone, and no amount of asking forgiveness would change that. She couldn't stay in Willow Springs and pretend that all would be well. With a shuddering sigh, she walked the rest of the way home.

***

Anna twisted a hankie through her fingers. "Emma, I'm worried. Rebecca hasn't gotten out of bed in two days, and she has some silly idea about moving to Willow Brook instead of marrying Eli."

"Marrying Eli?"

Anna laid her fingers over her lips. "*Jah*, she told *Datt* and Wilma that he asked her to marry him. But now, she said that she's changed her mind. Wilma is so set on the whole thing she keeps saying she is just nervous, and she'll come to her senses. Wilma has gone and started her a new wedding dress, and they haven't even been announced at church yet."

Emma sat on the stool at the counter and crossed her legs. "Eli might just be what our *schwester* needs."

Anna walked to the counter and straightened a jar of knitting needles. "You and I know that, but how do we convince Rebecca?"

Emma snickered. "She surely isn't going to take any advice from me. She can barely stand the sight of me. But if anyone can find a way around this, God can."

Anna smiled at Emma. Her *schwester's* faith was strong even though she often wondered if she and Samuel had veered off from their Old Order Amish traditions.

Anna shuffled a stack of patterns and placed them neatly in the holder near the cash register. "I doubt Rebecca puts much faith in God these days. We couldn't even get her to go to church yesterday. Even *Datt's* threats didn't budge her. She claimed she wasn't feeling well, but she doesn't have any signs of being ill."

"Anna, now you can't say that we don't know Rebecca's heart; only God does."

"I suppose, but nothing I say seems to make a mountain of beans. Please, can't you go talk to her? She might listen to you."

Emma slipped from the stool. "I doubt she'll even let me in her room, but I'll try."

Anna wrapped her arms around Emma's middle. "Oh, thank you."

***

Emma opened the kitchen door and snatched a cookie off the tray Wilma held in her hand. "I could smell these cookies clear out in the yarn shop."

"Emma, what a nice surprise. What do I owe this visit to?"

"Anna says Rebecca is feeling under the weather, and I thought I'd come and check on her."

Wilma set the tray on the table and wiped her hands on the towel flipped over her shoulder. "You're braver than I. She's been like a feral cat the last couple of days."

Emma poured a swig of milk in the bottom of a cup and washed down her cookie. "I've had more experience dealing with the likes of Rebecca. Please, don't hold it against her. She hasn't always been like this. Something happened around the time *Mamm* died that tripped her up. Hopefully, we can get to the bottom of it at some point. Until then, all we can do is keep praying for her."

Wilma sunk her hands in dishwater. "You have more patience with her than I do. I would just as soon stay far away. If she's not going to marry Eli, the best thing that girl can do is move to Willow Brook. I've had just about enough of her sour disposition."

"What a cruel thing to say." Emma's lip twitched.
Wilma didn't turn from her dishes. "What do you know? You don't have to live with her anymore."

"*Jah*, but it wouldn't hurt to show her some kindness."

"Kindness? You think that's all it would take?" Wilma gave a brittle laugh.

Emma caught her breath, and heat rose to her cheeks. "Jesus showed kindness even to the Samaritan woman at the well."

"TSK! I wouldn't know about such things. All I know is that girl is a hard one to like. Not sure how your father's kept her in line all these years. Besides, I have no intention to get in the middle of this ridiculous situation. If Eli Bricker is stupid enough to want to marry her, she best take her one and only shot at a husband. Otherwise, she's going to live a long fruitless life. And I'll tell you this. It won't be under this roof."

Quick tears came to Emma's eyes. *How could she speak so unkindly about Rebecca? Yes, her schwester was a bit hard to handle, but there was something much deeper at work with Rebecca. Why couldn't anyone see it? Especially her father.*

Emma knew she wouldn't get anywhere by talking to Wilma. She carried her cup to the sink and left the kitchen without responding to her stepmother's rant.

Her bare feet barely made a sound as she made her way up the hardwood stairs and to her *schwester's* room.

"Rebecca? It's Emma. May I come in?"

Rebecca let her breath out sharply. "If you must."

Emma pushed open the door. "Anna said you're feeling under the weather. Is there anything I can do for you?"

Rebecca pulled the pillow up over her head. "Not unless you can put an end to this day."

"Oh, it can't be that bad."

Emma pulled the pillow from her head. "How about we talk about whatever is bothering you?"

Rebecca pushed herself up and pulled her knees to her chest. "Why do you care?"

Emma sat on the edge of her bed and lifted her chin slightly. "There was a time when you shared everything with Anna and me. Why would this time be any different?"

"That was a long time ago, and much has changed since we were little girls. And besides, you have no idea what's going on in my life."

"*Nee*, I don't. Tell me."

Rebecca looked back at her in despair. "Why should I? So you can look down your nose at me again and prove that you have a perfect life with the perfect husband."

"That's a bit harsh, don't you think? I don't remember ever looking my nose down at you. If that's what you thought, then I owe you an apology because that was never my intention."

Rebecca pulled her nightdress over her knees and hugged them close to her chest. "Why do you bother with me?"

Rebecca's eyes flickered. "Because you're family, and that's what families do. They talk. They help each other through the tough spots in life. And they do as Jesus would do."

With a snip in her tone, Rebecca said, "And what would that be?"

Emma's eyes softened. "He'd love you."

Laying her head on her knees, Rebecca murmured, "First Mary, then Eli, and now you. I'm sick of hearing about God. He doesn't care a bit about me."

Emma laid her hand on her *schwester's* head. "If God has enough forgiveness and patience for me, He certainly has enough for you too."

"And all this talk of Jesus is going to get you into trouble."

Rebecca's eyes sparkled. "If that's what it takes to get His message heard, I'm up for the challenge."

Rebecca turned her face and laid her cheek on her knee as she studied her *schwester*. "Something is different with you and Samuel. What is it?"

Emma shifted and pushed a wrinkle out of her skirt. "If you'll let Him, God's ability to turn today's messes into tomorrow's masterpieces is amazing. But first, you have to forgive yourself for whatever is eating away at you and move on."

In not much more than a whisper, Rebecca responded, "Easy for you to say."

Emma stood. "*Jah, schwester,* it is. And when you're ready to fight your way back into the light, come find me. Then and only then will I show you the way through Jesus."

Rebecca leaned back against the headboard and flipped her legs out straight. "You best not let *Datt* hear you talk like that, or you'll be in more trouble than you're willing to face."

Emma leaned down and whispered, "All things truly do work together for good, no matter how impossible it may seem at first. And the times when I had felt the most alone and unloved were the times when He was developing depths of spiritual maturity I didn't possess yet. So, you see, *schwester* dear, you should be filled with gratitude, not griping during this season."

Face pinched, Rebecca pushed Emma aside and got up and walked to the window. "You have no idea!"

"Then help me understand."

Rebecca's cheeks flushed. "It's too late for me." Moving toward the door, she pushed Emma to the hallway and closed the door in her face.

CHAPTER 15

All the way home, Emma prayed for Rebecca. Her *schwester* was lost and hurting, and she hoped something, anything she might have said, would make a difference. As she walked past her mother-in-law's house, she waved at Ruth as she hung clothes.

From across the yard, she hollered, "Emma, I was just going to pour a glass of tea. Would you like to join me?"

Waving back, she replied, "I'm sure Katie can handle the bakery for a few more minutes."

Ruth dropped the bucket of clothespins in the empty basket at her feet and moved a loose hair off her forehead.

Locking her arm in her daughter-in-law's elbow, she patted her forearm. "It's been weeks since we've had a chance to chat much. This will be nice."

Emma clasped her hand over the older woman's hand. "It has been too long. I stay busy between the bakery and helping Katie and Daniel with Elizabeth. But I'm not complaining. God is good, *jah*?"

Ruth looked down at Emma's middle. "Perhaps soon you and Samuel will give Elizabeth a playmate?"

Emma struggled with what to say. She and Samuel had decided to follow Dr. Smithson's advice and wait two years before trying for another child. That was a decision they kept to themselves since they were going against tradition and preventing a pregnancy that could harm both the child and her.

She gave Ruth a rueful smile. "When God sees fit."

Ruth led Emma up the stairs and pointed to the two rocking chairs. "It's a beautiful day. It's a shame to spend it inside. Sit, I'll go get us a glass of tea."

From where Emma sat, she could see Samuel and Daniel working on a piece of equipment in the barn. Katie was sitting on the porch of the bakery playing with now six-month-old Elizabeth. Life was just about as perfect as things could be, but sitting there enjoying the day while her *schwester* was so troubled left her empty inside. Her mind was spinning with what she could do to help. But then again, it was all in God's hands, and there was nothing she could do but be a messenger.

She was reminded that it wasn't her place to change Rebecca's heart; that was God's job. All she could do was plant the seed. It would be up to Him to see it flourish and take root. Oh, how she prayed Rebecca could be free of whatever was bothering her.

Ruth pushed open the screen door with her hip, walked over, and handed Emma a cool drink. "Did you go visit your *Datt* and Wilma?"

"*Jah*, I hadn't seen my *schwesters* in a few days, so I walked down to check on them."

"All is well with Anna and Rebecca?"

"Rebecca is a little under the weather, but Anna is doing well."

Ruth took a sip of tea before asking, "I noticed Rebecca wasn't at church. I hope everything is okay?"

Emma sat her tea on the stand between them and sighed. "I think my *schwester's* problems are more emotional than health-related."

Both women set their chairs in motion and let the early June breeze fill the silence between them.

"Emma, do you think this would be a good time to give Rebecca your mother's gift?"

Emma brought her hands to her lips. "I'd forgotten about *Mamm's* gift. Oh, Ruth, this would be the perfect time for Rebecca to get a little piece of *Mamm*. It might just be what she needs."

"Do you want me to give it to her, or do you want to?"

"Oh, no, Ruth, it will mean more coming from you. Do you think you'd have time to give it to her today?"

From across the yard, they heard Katie call out. "Emma, can you come to take care of the customers? I need to put Elizabeth down for a nap."

Emma waved in Katie's direction and smiled before saying, "I best be going. Thanks for the tea, but more importantly, thank you for agreeing to see Rebecca. *Mamm's* shawl saw me through some of my roughest days after James died. I'll pray it will comfort Rebecca as well."

Emma picked up her pace toward Katie and Elizabeth. She only stopped for a second to kiss her niece's forehead before heading into the bakery.

***

Rebecca sat on the edge of her bed, brushing the snarls out of her hair from being in bed for two days. Emma's visit left her questioning so many things, so she wanted to take a walk to clear her head from the swirling thoughts. *Gratitude, not griping. I don't see one thing I have to be grateful for.*

Wilma's voice pierced the air. "Rebecca. Ruth Yoder is here to see you. Do you want me to send her up, or will you come down?"

Throwing her brush on the bed, she twisted her hair in a bun and pinned it at the back of her head. "I'll be down in a minute," she bellowed back.

Of all people, the last person she wanted to see was her mother's best friend. All Ruth would do was remind her that her mother was long gone, and she had no one to turn to when life was unbearable. She slipped on a fresh dress, pinned it closed, and headed down the stairs.

Ruth stood in the kitchen holding a white gift box. When she turned to face her, she held the package out in front of her.

Rebecca asked, "What's this?"

Ruth looked over her shoulder. "Wilma, do you mind if I speak to Rebecca in private for a minute?"

"Better you than me!"

Ruth's eyebrows furrowed, and she gave the woman a snarled look. "I won't keep her but a minute. Perhaps we will go sit on the porch; I wouldn't want to bother your bread-making."

"Suit yourself. I don't get much help from the girl anyways. Take as long as you please. Maybe you can talk some sense into her."

Ruth put her hand under Rebecca's elbow and guided her to the front porch. "Let's sit outside. There is a nice breeze to keep us cool."

Ruth pointed to the swing at the far end of the porch. "It's been a long time since I've sat on your mother's swing. How about we settle there?"

Rebecca steadied the box on her lap and asked, "Am I supposed to open this?"

"In a minute. Let me explain." Ruth laid her hand on the package and tapped it ever so gently. "The summer before your mother passed, she made each of you girls a little something to remember her by. She made me promise to present each of you her gift when I felt you needed it the most."

Rebecca's eyes welled with tears. "A gift for me, from *Mamm*?"

"*Jah*, for you. Please don't be upset with Emma, but she mentioned you had some things you were struggling with right now. And I felt this might be a good time for you to have a little piece of your *mamm*."

A sob lodged in the back of Rebecca's throat, and it closed around it, preventing her from speaking clearly. In a broken cry, she replied, "It's the … bes … best … time."

Ruth stood and placed her hand on Rebecca's shoulder. "I'd better be going. I have a list of chores to finish this forenoon. But please know that even though I can never replace your *mamm*, I'm always there to lend a shoulder to cry on if so need be."

Rebecca wiped a tear from her chin and swallowed hard. "I know."

Ruth put her arm around her. "Whatever has you so broken, please remember … joy comes from within. Dig deep into what you want out of life and make it happen. Don't wait for it to come to you. Go after it and hold on tight. Only then will you find relief from what troubles you."

Trembling slightly, Rebecca nodded. "*Denki*, Ruth."

Waiting until Ruth had made it off the porch, she gripped the sides of the box tightly. A small piece of her mother lay inside. It was like a dream playing out in slow motion as she removed the cover.

Folding back the pink tissue paper, she ran her hand along the tightly woven stitches of a crocheted shawl. She picked it up and held the soft fibers to her cheek.

She remembered watching her *mamm* sit on this same swing and work the tiny stitches. Little did she know the cascading shades of cream and white would one day belong to her.

Opening her eyes, she saw a pink envelope in the bottom of the box with her name written neatly across the front. Her mother's perfect penmanship brought a fresh tear to her eye as she retrieved the letter.

Rebecca,

My darling firstborn daughter. You came into this world crying loudly until you heard the whimper of your baby schwester. Always Anna's protector, I knew there would come a day when you, too, needed someone to come to your rescue.

My days are but short on this earth, and I wanted to leave a little something you could find comfort in once I was long gone.

Always my strong-willed child, you often tried to hide your pain. Perhaps you are afraid someone might recognize your weakness. Rebecca, please hear me. It is okay to be real around those who love you. If we can't be vulnerable around the people who mean the most to us, what kind of life is that?

I have no idea what troubles you on this day, but I know one person who can show you the way to true freedom from whatever pain you're running from. Jesus.

If Mary Bricker is still alive when you read this, please go to her. She is the one person in this community who will show you the truth.

I pray you will wrap yourself in this shawl on those days that seem too much to handle and remember me. Find comfort in knowing I left this world knowing my salvation was given freely. Just as it is for you. It doesn't matter what you've done. He loves you and is waiting for you to call His name. All you have to do is call on Him.

You may think you are hiding your pain, but your pain is hiding you. Put your faith in the one who washes all pain away. He will set you free.

All my love,

Mamm

Even though the sun settled on her shoulders, Rebecca wrapped the delicate piece around her. Closing her eyes and pulling herself into a hug, she imagined her mother's arms holding her tight as she thought. *Oh, Mamm, I need you so, it's been so hard without you. Every day seems harder than the next. You're so right. I am running from a pain so deep I'm not sure I'll survive. I don't understand what you're trying to tell me. Please, Mamm, I wish it were more apparent. I can't go to Mary, she's gone too. I miss your face, the sound of your voice. Please tell me what to do.*

When she opened her eyes, two doves had settled on the ground beneath the bird feeder. Her *mamm* told her doves always traveled in pairs. Where you saw one, you'd see another.

Tucking the letter back in its envelope, she placed the empty box on the floor and walked off the porch. Ignoring Wilma's voice from inside, she headed to the bakery. She had to find out if Emma had received a box from *Mamm* as well.

***

The wind blew traces of strawberries and sugar through the air the closer Rebecca got to Katie and Emma's Bakery. Just as she and Anna had dreams of opening a yarn shop, Katie and Emma spent their childhood dreaming of a bakery. Strawberry season was in full swing, and pies and tarts filled the shelves at the popular fruit stand that held the new bakery.

Letting a group of English tourists step before her, Rebecca slipped behind the counter and pulled Emma aside.

"What is it, Rebecca? I'm right in the middle of helping a customer."

"Please, Emma, I need to talk to you."

"Katie, can you take over for me for a minute?"

The dark-haired young woman set a piping bag down on the counter and wiped her hands on a towel. "Take your time. That was the last pie I needed to make for the day."

Emma pulled Rebecca into the kitchen and picked up a cup of water. "What's so important it couldn't wait ten minutes?"

Rebecca flipped the white shawl from her shoulders and held it out to her *schwester*. "Did you receive one of these too?" Emma sat on the stool at the counter and nodded.

"*Jah.*"

"When?"

"After we lost James."

"Has Anna?"

"Not that I'm aware of. I think Ruth was only to give them to us if she saw us struggling with something."

Rebecca pulled a stool close to Emma. "Did she write you a letter?"

"She did, and I can honestly say she helped save my life."

The words startled her. "How so?"

"I'm not sure what *Mamm* said to you, and you don't need to share that with me. But if she told you anything close to what she told me, you're on your way to discover some pretty amazing things."

She sat, looking pale. Leaning forward, she rested her chin in her hand and struggled not to cry. "Did she talk about Jesus?"

Emma's breath relaxed. "*Jah.*"

"And?"

"I discovered the truth."

Rebecca closed her eyes. "I'm trying to understand. But I don't see how Jesus can set me free."

Emma took a few moments to compile her thoughts before she answered. But before she did, the conversation with Samuel about how they had convinced Eli she wasn't in love with him rang loudly in her ear. Wrapping her feet around the legs of the stool, Emma braced herself for Rebecca's rebuttal.

"My battle was much different from yours, but *Mamm* pointed me toward the one person who could help me heal."

Rebecca switched elbows and started to tap her fingers on the worktable. "She said I needed to have faith in the one who could set me free." Rebecca sat up straight and asked, "I've been saved. How much more faith do I need?"

Emma watched her struggle to put all the pieces together, took in a deep breath, and let it out slowly before answering.

"Going through the motions of baptism and the traditions set in place by our forefathers means nothing."

Rebecca put her hand over Emma's mouth and whispered, "Shhh… you can't be saying things like that. What if someone hears you? They will excommunicate you!"

Grabbing Rebecca's hand, she leaned in closer. "Listen to me. The Bible doesn't lie. Neither does God. It's in black and white – if you believe in Jesus, you will have eternal life and be free from whatever you are carting around. That's what *Mamm* meant by having faith. You need to believe that your one true counselor, savior, and Messiah is Jesus Christ. It's who you put your faith in that matters in the end. It's not how you follow a set of rules or how good you are."

Emma took her index finger and tapped on Rebecca's chest ever so lightly. "It's not about the outward appearance or rituals this community is so set on. It's what is in here that counts. It will take a change of heart for you to truly grasp what *Mamm* is trying to teach you."

Rebecca pushed her hand away. "I'm scared for you. *Datt* will go to the bishop if he gets word of how you're talking."

"I don't care about that right now. All I care about is showing you that Jesus is the answer." Emma looked at the line of customers building up. "I have to go help Katie, but before I do, you need to think about this... confession will set you free."

Emma rose and looked at her apologetically. "If you get it out in the open, it will lose its power over you."

Rebecca was left sitting alone to ponder her *schwester's* words. A heaviness pushed at her chest, wanting to escape as she thought. *Could Emma be right? Was it time she was honest with herself and with God? Oh, how she wished she understood all the things Mary, Mamm, and now Emma were trying to show her.*

As she walked out of the bakery, she said a prayer that her *datt* and the bishop wouldn't get wind of what Emma was saying. But if what she said was true, then all the lies, secrets, and deception could be forgiven.

Lost deep in thought, she stepped out in front of a car. A sudden beep forced her to jump away from its bumper. As she waved at the woman behind the wheel, she focused on a large sticker pasted to the side of the vehicle. YOUR PAST DOESN'T DEFINE YOUR FUTURE.

CHAPTER 16

Eli caught his breath as he watched Rebecca step out in front of the car, maneuvering its way into the parking lot. He chose to stay hidden in the shadows of the work shed as soon as he saw her walk down the bakery steps. It had been a couple of days since he let her run away. It pained him to think she carried around something so hurtful it would keep her from finding true happiness. After stewing for days, he left the farm in search of the one person who might help him find a way to get through to her.

Samuel wiped his hands on a red shop rag and walked up to stand beside him. Nodding his head in Rebecca's direction, he asked, "She's wound pretty tight. Are you sure you want to untangle that knotted-up mess?"

Eli stepped back to make sure he stayed hidden. "I look at it as making an investment in my future."

"I suppose you're right. Those Byler girls do get under your skin. Ain't so?"

Eli stood up straighter. "I need to convince her there is more to life than the box she's put herself in."

"Well, you best figure it out soon. Emma says she's planning on leaving for the job in Willow Brook next week."

Reaching for the brim of his straw hat, Eli pulled it tighter on his forehead. "She's not going anywhere if I have anything to say about it."

As he started to walk from the shed, Samuel stated, "Don't forget our meeting tomorrow night at eight. Daniel and Katie will be there along with Emma and me. There is a good chance that Henry and Maggie Schrock are joining us. We have to discuss what we will do if word leaks out about our bible studies. Please don't bring your buggy. We don't want to bring any attention to the house. We will be meeting in the basement, so no one driving by will see the lights.

"Henry Schrock? He was just appointed minister. How did that come about?"

"He's been talking with Daniel. Word has it that his community in Elkhart, Indiana, was much different from here. Daniel said he's having a hard time conforming to our Old Order ways, which are so different from how he was raised."

"I bet now that he's a minister and in the middle of everything, he's figuring out what we already know."

"*Jah*, things are going to get a little hairy around here before too long, and we need to be prepared." Samuel slapped Eli and the shoulder. "See you tomorrow?"

"*Jah*."

Samuel stopped and replied in a hushed tone. "Be certain where Rebecca's loyalty lies before you breathe a word about any of this to her."

Clearly, that was a message that didn't sit well with Eli. "I'm fully aware of where we all need to stand on these issues."

Samuel hesitated before answering. "I just know how vindictive Rebecca has been in the past. If she thinks for one minute that she can use something against Emma, she'll use it no questions asked."

Eli knew Samuel was right, but he still couldn't stand to hear any ill words spoken about the woman who had her heart all entangled with his. "We all need to be trusting in God, and that includes Rebecca. You just worry about Emma and let me take care of Becca."

Samuel smiled slightly. "Becca?"

Eli gave a nod and left without another word.

***

Eli set his buggy in the direction of the Feed & Seed. So much of him wanted to follow Rebecca down Mystic Mill Road. Still, the determination in her step left him turning the opposite direction. He needed more time to think and ponder the words he needed to convince her to stay.

***

Rebecca stood at the end of Eli's driveway and looked around the farm. His buggy horse was not in the padlock, and the barn door where he stored his cart was open. As far as she could tell, he was gone. Did she dare go inside the house? She wanted to feel a sense of Mary and wished she could talk to her.

Why had *Mamm* told her to speak to Mary? All this talk of truth and forgiveness and being set free was swirling around in her head. Wrapping her mother's shawl around her shoulders tighter, she headed to the house.

Guilt assaulted her as she pushed the kitchen door open. Shame filled her, but only for a second until her need for peace took over her better judgment. The kitchen sink was stacked with dirty dishes, and she couldn't help but smile as she thought. *Things never change.*

Mary's sweater still hung on the peg by the front door as she walked through the living room. The woman's presence clung to every part of the home, much like the pleats in the blue curtains. From its blue doors to its white clapboard siding, every house in Willow Springs looked the same. However, the secrets hidden behind each door were what kept them separated, even in Mary and Eli's home.

Sinking down in Mary's chair, she laid her head back and looked out into the kitchen. Sitting on the top of the hutch in the corner of the room was the bible she'd seen Eli place out of sight. She closed her eyes and thought. *Don't do it, Rebecca! It's one thing to walk in his house when he's not here. But looking through his private things?*

Opening her eyes, she swallowed hard and moved toward the hutch. She reached up and grasped the black leather Bible with a shaky hand. She had never held an English bible, and her father's German Bible was large and not comfortable in her hand. Let alone she'd never learned to read German. She relied on her father and the ministers to interpret the old language. The smooth cover rested easily in her palm as she fingered the fine paper inside with her other hand. Tucked in between the pages were notes and pages marked with string.

The tiny hairs on her forearms tingled as she read a few notes Eli had written in the margin. An English version was strictly forbidden but holding the book that held Eli's most private thoughts left her wanting more of him.

The cold floor seeped through her bare feet, and a strange feeling overcame her clear to the top of her head. When her thumb met a folded yellow lined piece of paper tucked tightly between the pages, she stopped when she saw her name.

She fought the urge to open the sheet of paper. Instead, her eyes followed the underlined text. THEN YOU WILL KNOW THE TRUTH, AND THE TRUTH WILL SET YOU FREE.

The book slid from her hands, as did the letter with her name on it. She couldn't run fast enough from the house. Turning the corner, she ran smack dab into Eli's arms. His bold shoulders absorbed her body without even losing his footing.

She swung from his hold, but not before he grabbed her arm and pulled her back into his chest. "Oh, no, you don't. I'm not letting you run away so fast this time."

Rebecca sighed heavily. "Please, Eli, let me go."

"*Nee!* I'm not letting you go. You came here for a reason. What is it?"

"I'm sorry, I shouldn't have come."

"But you did, and I'm not letting you leave until we talk."

He pulled her in close and whispered, "Why are you running from me?"

She placed her hands on his chest. "Because you deserve better."

He lifted her chin until their eyes met. "Better than what? A woman so set in running from what she truly wants because she thinks her sins are worse than anyone else's?"

"They are?"

He rested his forehead on hers. "But you're wrong. We all have secrets and sins that hold us captive."

She tried to push him back. "Not like mine."

He dropped his hold, took her by the hand, and led her into the house. His bible and notes were scattered on the floor when he stepped inside. He didn't say a word but stooped down, picked them up, and placed them on the table. Pointing to the chair nearest his at the head of the table, he said, "Please sit; I want to read you something."

"Eli, please."

"Please, Becca, hear me out. If what I'm about to read doesn't make sense, I promise I'll let you go home."

For the first time in months, she had no more fight left in her. Exhausted, she sat in the chair and folded her hands on her lap. She waited for him to question her about the book on the floor, but he said nothing.

Taking his seat beside her, he turned toward the back of the book. "This comes from John 8, Verse 12. *When Jesus spoke again to the people, he said, "I am the light of the world. Whoever follows me will never walk in darkness, but will have the light of life."*

She held onto his every word as he continued to read through the chapter in the Book of John, until he concluded with: *"If you hold onto my teachings, you are my disciples. Then you will know the truth, and the truth will set you free."*

Rebecca frowned and dropped her head. She couldn't look into his eyes; they held so much hope. More than she had for herself.

Seconds turned into minutes, and the only sound was the constant tick-tock from the clock on the wall. Not until he laid his hand over hers, still clenched together in her lap, did she look up. With a gentle squeeze to her fingers, he said, "If we confess. He forgives."

A small gasp escaped her lips when his words hit such a tender spot. In an instant, a buzzing took place in her ears, and she was afraid she might pass out before she answered, "Not me. Even if God does, you won't."

"*Jah*, Becca, I will."

Eli moved to the floor and knelt beside her. "You don't give me enough credit. Please, let me be the light that shines brightness into your darkness. We all fail at times, but I promise you I will not fail you. Let me show you all the things no one ever explained to you."

Her tears dropped on her hand, and he picked it up and kissed them away. He leaned in and rested his head on hers. She closed her eyes and let his voice carry them away. She had never heard a man pray out loud before. Still, the husky tone of his voice mingled together with a sureness she'd never experienced before; he lifted her up in prayer. Without any hesitation, she knew more than anything else she'd ever known; Eli Bricker knew God, and God knew Eli Bricker.

He finished with: *"Heavenly Father, open Becca's heart and show her that those you want to use are those who are not perfect. In Jesus' name, Amen."*

Listening to him read from the bible to his outward boldness of petitioning God on her behalf left her speechless. At that moment, she knew she needed to take a chance on love and pour her heart out to the one and only man she'd ever loved. If Eli trusted and had faith in what God could do, she wanted the same reassurance.

She didn't budge. She didn't want the connection they had to leave. He had a hold on her heart, and she felt the rough edges fall away. Without opening her eyes, she whispered, "You may not want anything to do with me once you hear what I've done."

He moved his lips to her forehead and whispered back, "Try me."

She moved her head away from his, twisted from his grip, and walked to the window. When he tried to follow, she quickly said, "Please stay. I can't bear to watch the disappointment on your face."

He moved to his chair. Rebecca crossed her arms over her chest and stared out the window. Then began to tell him her darkest secrets.

"I could have saved Billy Gingerich from getting hit by that truck. But I didn't. I ignored his mother's screams and let him run past me because I was so wrapped up in myself."

She waited for Eli to say something, anything, but when he didn't, she continued to look out the window and kept going.

"Samuel knew what I did and didn't tell anyone. He waited for me to confess, and when I didn't, it'd been too long, so I blackmailed him into lying to you."

The air in the room was still. A chill ran down Rebecca's spine right before she felt his calloused hands rest on her shoulders. Her back stiffened at his touch. She wouldn't allow herself to relax until she told it all.

"It was my turn to be with my mother, but I couldn't sit a minute longer, so I went to the barn. She died all by herself because of my own selfish desires."

"Samuel and Emma lost James because of me. God used their baby as a sacrifice to my sin."

Eli took a deep breath but didn't say a word as he blew it out close to her ear.

"Your grandmother died alone. You trusted me to care for her, but again I chose myself over doing what was right."

She turned and faced him. "I'm not worthy of God or anyone else."

Eli pulled her into his chest and rested his chin on the top of her head. "Becca, no one can know when it's someone's time to go. And whether you were there or not, it's not your fault."

She raised her hands to his chest and buried her face in her palms. "I'm certain it was God's way of punishing me."

He pulled her hands away from her face. "You're wrong. God doesn't punish like that. He loves us, and that includes you."

She looked up into his eyes. "But you? Can you love me knowing all this?"

"I've never stopped loving you."

Through a quick blush, she asked, "But all the warnings my *datt* gave you?"

Fighting back the tears, Rebecca looked at him with pleading eyes. "I even came into your house uninvited."

His face filled with compassion. "If I remember correctly, it's your house too."

In a quieter tone she said, "Still, I had no right."

266

Until that moment, she had no way of knowing how Eli would react to her confession. But his arms engulfed her, and she relaxed under his embrace.

His cheek rested on the side of her head, and he asked, "Is there anything else? Now is the time to get everything out in the open."

Trembling, she knew she had to tell one more secret that wasn't hers to tell. Eli must have sensed her hesitation because he leaned back and lifted her chin. "What is it, Becca?"

"I know *Mommi* Mary's secret."

Her eyes burned with tears in anticipation of revealing the secret that ruined his family's internal relationship. "It's horrible, and I can see why Noah wanted her to take it to the grave."

Eli sank down in the nearest chair. "I hate the thought of you having to carry around such knowledge, but I'm not sure I want to hear what my grandfather felt was so important that he wanted to keep it hidden."

Rebecca nodded. "She loved your father and tried to protect him, much like Noah protected her. Only your father couldn't see it that way. He blamed her, and I'm certain that came once your father moved to Lancaster."

Eli held her gaze. "Why do you think that?"

She sat down in the chair beside him and picked up his hand. "I think your great-grandfather brainwashed your father into believing things that weren't true."

Eli rested his arms on the back of the table and stretched his legs out in front of him. "Will anything good come from knowing the truth?"

She crossed her legs and pondered his question. After a few seconds, she responded, "Not for you, because you loved your grandmother unconditionally. But it might help your father understand why he couldn't see his parents for what they truly were."

"Then maybe I need to know. My father holds a great deal of resentment for them both. Maybe he could get some relief from the bitterness he holds."

"Oh, he's going to hold bitterness, I'm sure, but it won't be for Mary and Noah."

Despair filled him as Rebecca explained how his great-grandfather had taken advantage of Mary, leaving her with child. To prevent her any more embarrassment Noah took the blame and quietly moved her to Willow Springs.

Eli was confident the pain on his face was the same as the agony reflected on Rebecca's as she shared what she knew.

He leaned forward and rested his elbows on his knees. "What am I supposed to do with that?"

Rebecca moved closer. "Maybe take it to God?"

A slight smile escaped his lips. "There's hope for you yet, Becca Byler."

She put a hand on his arm. "Can I change my answer about marrying you?"

"Only after you hear me out. I have a confession to make myself. Only then will I let you make your decision. You may not want anything to do with me after hearing what I have to share. It will change your life forever."

She patted his arm. "I doubt I'll change my mind, but if you can forgive me, then whatever you have to say makes no difference in my world."

She noticed he didn't look at her while he struggled with finding the words that rolled around in his head.

"There's a good chance if you marry me, we will be excommunicated and asked to leave the church."

Rebecca's response was confident. "Eli Bricker, I will follow you anywhere."

"I don't think you fully understand. I have been attending private bible studies with Samuel and Daniel. Even Emma and Katie have been joining in. We have been studying God's word and learning so many truths that have changed the way we look at our eternal salvation and what God has planned for our lives."

"Does this have anything to do with what is going on with Samuel and Emma? If so, I want to be part of it."

His face went white and bleak. "It may mean you won't be able to speak to your father or Anna. You've already been baptized, so we will be shunned for certain."

Eli saw the determination on her face. "Things are going to change, but I can't promise you it will be easy. The elders of our community will not accept us."

"Please, Eli, I want what Emma has. I want to know the God that's shown you so much grace that you can forgive me as well. I want to truly know the God who loves me even more than my own father does."

Eli took her in his arms and brushed a soft kiss on her cheek. "I promise to protect you and cherish you forever, but what I'm asking you to do will affect your life forever."

She laid her hand on his cheek. "I'm tired of facing things alone. I eagerly want to hear all you have to say. If that means

I must leave my old life behind, again, I'll follow you anywhere."

CHAPTER 17

The following two weeks were a complete blur of activity. Neither Eli nor Rebecca had another chance to speak about going against the *Ordnung*. After Eli spoke to Jacob, Wilma returned to work on wedding plans with Anna's help.

While it was highly uncommon for a wedding to occur during the summer months, Eli got special permission from Rebecca's father after sharing the stipulation to keep his grandmother's farm.

Until Rebecca overheard a conversation between Wilma and her father, she hadn't thought twice about what lay ahead. Walking in on their private conversation initiated a pretty intense warning from her father. After that, she was more anxious to get out from under her father's roof and away from Wilma and her meddling ways.

Standing in her room on the morning of her wedding, she allowed Anna to help her pin her new royal blue dress together at the waist.

Anna removed a straight pin she held between her lips and asked, "Are you nervous?"

"Excited, I guess."

"How about you? Are you excited to be one of my side sitters with Ben Kauffman?"

Anna curled her lip upward. "I've thought of nothing else the last few days."

"Whatever happened between Ben's *bruder,* Simon, and you?"

"Now, *schwester,* today is not the day to speak of such things. This is your day, not mine."

Rebecca let Anna help her put on her new white apron and replayed her father's warning in her head.

***

Wilma dried her hands on a towel and lowered her voice. "It's best she gets out from under your care before the bishop gets word of what's going on. It wouldn't look good for you if you had to shun not one of your daughters but two. Especially if she still lived under your roof. We can only hope Anna doesn't fall prey to their influence."

Rebecca came up the basement steps unnoticed and stopped in the doorway when her father's eyes met hers.

"What do you know about meetings being held at your *schwester's*?"

Without answering his direct questions, she was quick to respond. "I haven't attended any meetings at Emma's. Why do you ask?"

Wilma pulled a chair out and let out a sharp "TSK."

Rebecca's heart picked up a beat as she waited for her father to probe further.

"Eli's been seen spending a good amount of time at Samuel's and Daniel's lately. Do you know what that might be about?"

Swift with her response, she said, "They're friends. Why would it be strange they spend time together?"

Her father gripped the arms of his chair. "I'd think they'd have better use of their time."

Wilma gave a slight shrug. "You're awful lucky your father could petition for this early wedding. I would hope you wouldn't do anything that might tarnish his position."

Rebecca looked back at her and bit her tongue. No amount of pushing Wilma's buttons the day before her wedding would prove to solve anything. "I've been too busy the last couple of weeks to pay any attention to where Eli's been." While it wasn't a lie, she surely wasn't going to divulge the little she did know.

Her father tipped his mouth in a bitter frown. "It's best to remember that Eli just switched his church membership to this district, and the both of you are now baptized members of this community."

Her mouth flattened, and she swallowed hard at his warning. "*Jah*," was all she could mutter as she walked through the kitchen and up the stairs to her room.

***

That was last night, and she spent a good part of her evening on her knees begging once again for God's forgiveness. There wasn't anything that would keep her from marrying Eli, not even a stern warning from her father.

***

"Rebecca, did you hear me?"

"*Jah* and be careful with those pins!"

Anna could tell something was bothering her *schwester,* and she hoped it was just wedding jitters. "You seem wound tighter than a rabbit caught in a cage. What are you so deep in thought about this morning?"

Rebecca took Anna's hand. "Please promise me no matter what happens, you'll always find a way to see me."

Anna squeezed her hand. "What's that supposed to mean? We run the yarn shop together; why wouldn't we see each other? Do you have plans to start a family right away?"

A nervous giggle escaped Rebecca's lips. "Only God knows that. I was just worried we wouldn't get to spend as much time together."

Anna tipped her chin. "Who are you, and what have you done with my *schwester*?"

"I don't have any idea what you are referring to."

Anna reached up and pulled Rebecca's new starched white *kapp* in place and asked, "Come on now. The *schwester* I know was a bit tattered and torn. This person is softer around the edges, and if that is what marrying Eli did to you, I need to thank him personally."

Rebecca grabbed her hand and pulled her toward the door. "We better get to Ruth and Levi's before the guests start to arrive. Eli might think I changed my mind if he doesn't see me there early."

Anna pulled back. "So, you're not going to answer me? What has gotten into you today?"

Rebecca grinned her way. "I suppose you need to thank Eli for the change you see in me. He helped me see things aren't always as bad as I've made them out to be over the years."

Anna rolled her eyes. "Where has he been my whole life? If I knew all it would take was for you to fall in love, I would have pushed Eli under your nose a lot sooner."

Anna let Rebecca drag her from the room, and they chatted giddily as they walked next door to the Yoder's where the wedding would take place.

The day was full of firsts. Every hurdle Rebecca thought she had to climb herself was replaced with Eli taking charge and being by her side. She was touched by his tenderness and attentiveness throughout the day. Even the solemn looks of her father and Wilma did little to dampen her joyful mood. By the time the wedding ended close to eleven that evening, Eli had bent down and whispered in her ear, "I think it's time to take my wife home. Are you ready?"

A smile filled her face, and a flash of heat rose from her neck and settled on her cheeks. She savored every minute of their twenty-minute walk back to the Bricker Farm. They would return early the next day to help clean up from the day-long activity, but at that moment and for the rest of her life, she would treasure the feel of Eli's strong, calloused hand in hers.

***

The warm soil felt good beneath Rebecca's bare feet as she worked the earth in the garden. When her hoe caught a clump of Mary's Johnny Jump-ups, she fell to her knees and gently buried the roots. She fell back on folded knees and looked around. The July sun beat on her back, and she marveled at how everything looked well and alive under Eli and her care. She had spent weeks working on Mary's gardens and prayed she was smiling down on her from above.

Only when her father's buggy stopped alongside the fence where Eli was working did the hairs on the back of her arms stand up. Being too far to hear their conversation, she knew her husband's stance was one of concern.

***

The steady clip-clop of an approaching buggy alerted Eli's attention away from the sheep he tended to in the pasture. When the metal wheels stopped behind him, he released the young lamb from his grip and turned toward the road.

Eli walked to the fence and waited until Jacob stepped down from his brown-topped buggy.

The lines etched on the old man's face deepened. "I fear trouble is at your doorstep."

Eli took his straw hat off and wiped his brow before returning the sweat-laden hat back to his head. "Trouble? What kind of trouble might that be?"

Eli's face burned hot. No doubt he knew what was coming, but Jacob would need to spell it out clearly before he yielded to his comment.

Stiffening his shoulders, Jacob asked, "Did you not promise to obey the teaching of our forefathers?"

Balancing his foot on the bottom rung of the picket fence, Eli leaned on his knee. "And didn't you agree to teach your church the ways of the Lord?"

Eli watched Jacob's neck turn red, and the vein that ran alongside his temple twitched. He stared at him for a moment, unsure if he should interfere with Jacob's thoughts. Who could blame the older man's confusion at Eli's rebuttal? But Eli wasn't about to let Jacob Byler intimidate him, even if he was Rebecca's father.

"I would hope and pray you would adhere to the traditions of our community when you married my daughter. We are a unified people, and change comes with a price. *Jah*?"

Eli stood up straight and didn't take his eyes from his father-in-law's. "And what would that price be?"

Jacob clenched his jaw and then let out an exasperated sigh. After coughing, he wiped his hand on his trouser leg and continued, "I'd prefer Rebecca not work at the yarn shop."

Silence pressed between them until Eli replied. "That is Rebecca's business. How can you forbid her to work?"

"My word is final. Until we clear up these rumors that are landing on your doorstep, I forbid Rebecca to work with Anna."

Eli was quick to stand his ground. "Then I'll move the shop here to the farm."

"You'll do no such thing unless you're prepared to buy me out. I footed the bill for that shop and its contents. Are you in a position to do so?"

The muscle in Eli's jaw flexed as he clenched his teeth. Jacob knew he sunk every penny he had into fixing up his farm. "Not at the moment, but I'll find a way."

Jacob turned and climbed back inside his waiting buggy. Before he pulled away, he added, "There is one quick and easy way to settle this matter."

"What's that?"

"Put a stop to these rumors and step into obedience to the *Ordnung.*"

There was no way Eli didn't understand what Jacob was referring to. The man had just given him an ultimatum. He could succumb to their Old Order ways, or he would be forced to forbid Rebecca from running the yarn shop. Both seemed impossible compromises.

Jacob snapped the reins and looked back at Eli one last time before pulling back out in the road. "You're destined to hell if you choose to turn your back on your promises."

Without replying to the old man's threat, he thought. *God has a purpose for my life, and a few wordy threats won't deter me from the path God's put me on.*

***

Rebecca placed the hoe and rake in the wheelbarrow and moved it to the back of the house. From the open window, the chime on the kitchen clock rang five. A hollow void filled her stomach as she watched the two men from afar. Something was amiss, and she was dying to know why her husband's stance took on a protective guard.

After moving to the kitchen, she washed her hands and kept a steady eye on the road. If the conversation had been meant for her, she would have been invited, but rarely did such things happen. The man of the house would be held responsible for all household members.

Her father pulled away and instantly encouraged his buggy horse to pick up his trot. It was unusual for her *datt* to push the old mare so quickly. Hoping Eli would return to the house, she promptly went to work, pulling out the potato salad and ham slices she had prepared earlier. With no breeze flowing through the house's open windows, she gathered things to carry out to the picnic table under the maple tree in the front yard.

Keeping an eye on the barn for Eli, she snapped the checkered tablecloth on the table and neatly set supper out. Returning to the house only once to pour two glasses with water, she returned to find Eli straddling a bench at the table.

Nodding her head in the direction of the road, she asked. "What did my father want?"

Eli glanced at the road. "He came with a warning."

"Oh, no, that doesn't sound good."

Eli patted the bench beside him. "Please sit. We need to talk." He proceeded to tell her everything, along with his refusal to permit her to work at the yarn shop.

"But how can he forbid me to work? That is my shop, not his."

Eli reached for her hand. "Did you pay for the construction cost?"

"*Nee.*"

"Did you pay for any of the inventory to get it opened?"

284

"*Nee.*"

"Have you contributed anything to the overall maintenance of the building other than preparing the fiber for sale?"

"*Nee.*"

"Then I'm sorry, my love. You don't own that shop. He does."

Her mouth trembled. "Can he really do this?"

"I'm afraid he can. But I don't want you to worry. I'll figure out a way for you to keep the shop, or you'll open a new one here."

"But what about the rumors he hinted at. Did he tell you exactly what he'd heard?"

"*Nee*, he didn't. But I have to assume the way he warned me of hell, he's caught wind of our bible studies. Or he at least suspects we are pushing the lines of our baptismal promises."

Rebecca's lips quivered. "This is just the beginning, isn't it?"

He pulled her close and rested his head near her ear. "I've been seeking answers long before your father came into my life. Not one of the ministers or even the bishop could confidently answer my questions. Only Henry Schrock gave me the time of day when I pointed out some scripture for clarity." He paused and turned her head, so he could look into her eyes. "God never promised it would be easy to follow Him. But I have faith that we are on a path that will glorify Him the most. I'm not giving up my bible in exchange for a list of man-made rules and traditions. Even if that means you'll lose the yarn shop, and we are asked to leave the church."

She took in a small gasp and reached for his hand. "Even if it means I lose the yarn shop, I promised to follow you, and I trust you will do what is best for our family."

Eli bowed his head and prayed over their meal, including a short prayer for Jacob. When he lifted his head, he stated, "Your father is only following what he's been taught his whole life. Please don't hold anything against him. He was given a great responsibility to this district that he must abide by. Which includes keeping us in line."

Rebecca put a scoop of salad on his plate, handed him two bread slices for his ham, and asked, "Have you read the German Bible?"

Holding his sandwich to his mouth, he answered, "I don't understand a word of it, and my guess is most of the ministers don't either. We're encouraged to read from a bible we don't understand. And the bishop doesn't understand why so many of our youth have questions."

Rebecca took a sip of water and thought about his response. "*Datt* always said to read too much was giving the devil a way to eat away at our soul."

Eli snickered and shook his head. "That comes from fear of the unknown. Maybe I need to show your *datt* a thing or two about what scripture really says."

The bite of salad Rebecca held in her mouth went down wrong, and she coughed. When she finally was able to wash it down with another sip of water, she said, "Good luck with that."

Rebecca played with a fork of salad on her plate and tipped her head in his direction. "He's also been known to say, 'Unified people hide their knowledge for the sake of the community. It's what keeps our kind separated from the world. When too much learning seeps in, the community is sure to divide'."

"Well, he might be onto something there."

"Ya know what, Eli?"

"What's that?"

"I think it's about time this community gets stirred up some."

He snickered at her sureness. "That's good; because it's going to take a whole lot of God to change the hearts of our people."

She leaned into his arm. "If God can change this woman, he can certainly change the hearts and minds of the surrounding people."

He elbowed her, forcing her to drop her fork. "Let's see if you still feel the same way when Bishop Weaver shows up on our front porch."

She sat up straight and held her sandwich a few inches from her mouth. "I can honestly say I'm not worried. Sure, I might be forbidden to see Anna for a short while, but I still have Emma and Katie. And by the sounds of it, perhaps Henry Schrock's wife, Maggie."

He leaned in kissed her cheek. "Who is this girl? Look at you being content with spending time with Emma."

Compliments came few and far between; hence they were considered prideful. But she couldn't help but blush at her husband's kind words. "I suppose when Samuel re-baptized me in Willow Creek four weeks ago, more of my old thoughts washed down the stream than I realized."

They let her words mix together with the evening nesting of birds in the tree overhead before she added, "I know I'm far from perfect, and at times I still have ugly thoughts I have to push away. But when they get close to landing on my tongue, all I have to do is envision Jesus hanging on the cross."

Jake, their sheepdog, barked at the three buggies, one after the other, as they pulled in their driveway.

Eli stood, wiped his mouth on a napkin and stepped over the bench. "So, it begins."

CHAPTER 18

Rebecca hung back, gathering up their supper dishes as Eli met their visitors. Samuel and Emma were the first to secure their horse to the hitching post and stepped down from their enclosed buggy. Daniel and Katie, followed by Henry and Maggie.

Each face was stricken with an eternal struggle. Emma headed to the picnic table and helped her carry the remnants of the meal to the house. No words were needed as both *schwester's* worked in silence.

Rebecca let Emma step in front of her and followed her to the house. Stopping in the middle of the driveway, Rebecca looked from the porch to the road. An overwhelming feeling of life as she knew it was slipping from her fingers. Remarkably, she wasn't worried. In the distance, a storm ripped away at the landscape, and a crack of lightning hit a lone pine tree in the pasture. The quick flash of light, followed by a blast of fire, tumbled the tree to the ground.

The sound alerted Eli, and he and the men worked quickly to shelter the horses in the barn. The ground shook under the tree's weight, and Emma and Rebecca ran to the house.

Katie held open the kitchen door, and Emma's face convulsed briefly. "Did you feel that?"

Katie's eyes flashed. "Please tell me that wasn't a warning sign of what's to come." Maggie took dishes from Rebecca and replied. "A freak act of nature, ain't so?"

Katie worked on lighting the kerosene lamp over the table and asked Rebecca. "So, did your *datt* pay a visit to you and Eli today?"

"*Jah*. You too?"

Katie looked troubled. Rebecca heard it in her voice and saw it in her hands. All eyes switched back to her when she asked Emma. "I couldn't hear exactly what *Datt* said to Eli, but I could tell it wasn't good."

"*Jah*, me either, but Samuel told me everything he said. Samuel is certain we will be called in front of the church."

Katie moved her hand to her mouth to hide a moan, and Maggie added, "Jacob asked Henry to meet with him and Bishop Weaver in the morning."

Maggie added a pot of water to the stove. "If they do, I'm confident they'll question us about our baptismal oath."

Katie sank down in a chair, opened a tea bag, and draped it in a cup. "I didn't even understand those promises. They were all in German, and who could understand a word of it anyway?"

Emma leaned over the sink and watched the men run across the yard. "Here they come now. Rebecca, you better get a couple of towels."

Taking a seat beside Katie, Maggie added, "For sure and certain we'll be reminded we'll go in the fire for eternity."

Katie sucked in a long breath and covered her eyes with the palms of her hands. "I knew this day would come. I just didn't think it would happen so fast."

Eli was the first in the door and took the towel Rebecca handed him before she stepped behind him to give one to Samuel, Daniel, and Henry.

Eli dried his head. "That came up quick." Draping the towel over Rebecca's arm, he asked, "So I assume we all got a visit from Jacob today?"

After handing the wet towel back to Rebecca, Samuel took a seat at the table. "*Jah*. He gave me little room to speak, but his warning was straightforward. We were not to search for the truth, other than what is taught on Sunday morning."

Daniel pulled a chair out beside Katie and flipped it around to straddle it. Leaning his elbows on the chair back, he added, "My warning was much the same. I was not to lead my family in any way that would go against the *Ordnung*. If I did, there would be no hope for our salvation. And we were destined to do the devil's work."

Maggie pulled a chair out and patted its seat for Henry to sit beside her. Wrapping his arm around the back of Maggie's chair, Henry stated, "My warnings were more intense. It hasn't even been a year since I've been appointed minister. I'm sure my meeting with the bishop tomorrow will come at a price."

Maggie rested her hand on her husband's knee. "God always has a purpose. And all you did was ask questions that neither Bishop Weaver nor the other ministers could answer."

Daniel piped in. "Precisely why we started to seek for our own answers. You all know I'll be blamed for all of this. I'm certain the bishop is regretting ever granting me church membership. I'm the reason you all have questions in the first place."

Samuel leaned back in his chair. "God wanted us to see the truth that they have the salvation message wrong. The church members can no faster get to heaven by their works than I can bring that burned tree back to life. And besides, there's not one person in this district that can claim they will ever be good enough to go to heaven."

Katie wilted against the back of her chair. "Will they bring us all in front of the church to repent?"

Daniel tipped his chin in her direction. "What do we have to confess about? We've done nothing wrong."

Even Maggie's stomach was in turmoil with the possibility. "You know to the members of our church, it's a sin to study an English bible, especially in a group setting. And sin is only forgiven by a public confession."

Henry reached for a cookie off the plate in the middle of the table. "I've been studying the oath we took, and I believe an oath should be based on the truth."

Maggie passed the box of tea bags around the table. "We looked long and hard at the words of our promises and translated them the best we could from German to English."

Henry waited until his wife had finished before adding, "We promised to adhere to the standards of the church and to help administer them according to God's Word. What we promised was to follow a list of man-made rules and traditions that can't be found in the bible."

Emma agreed. "When our Mennonite friends explained that to us, Samuel and I were shocked. When I joined the church and agreed to those things, I didn't understand them. Now that I know my hope comes only from Jesus, those promises I made to the Amish church mean nothing."

Katie crossed her legs and bounced her tea bag up and down in her mug. "I believe everything Daniel has shared with me. I know our future is uncertain, and I trust God's plan. Still, I'm struggling with breaking my promises to God and the church."

Emma moved to sit next to Katie and took her hand. "So did I. Until I repented and asked God to forgive me, I was surrounded by guilt. But once I did, I was released from that heavy burden."

Rebecca stood and poured more cream into the pitcher on the table. "The last couple of months have been freeing for me. Eli's taught me so much in such a short time that I don't ever want to go back to a way of life where I need to be controlled to stay in God's good graces."

Katie followed Rebecca with her eyes and asked, "But what about Anna and the yarn shop? Jacob warned Daniel that the community won't shop at the bakery. I assume that will be the same for the yarn shop. You won't be able to work with your *schwester*."

Emma responded to Katie's question. "I'm not giving up on Anna just yet."

Samuel snickered and nodded his head in Rebecca's direction. "I didn't think I'd ever see a day when you stood among us. If God can work on your heart, I'm certain Anna won't be far behind."

Emma patted Katie's hand. "Stop worrying. All we need to do is keep pointing people to Jesus through God's word. He will do the rest."

Daniel added, "And that means He will direct our path to whatever is to come. Even if that means being put in the *bann*."

Henry took a sip from his mug before responding. "Look, we're in this together and we'll never be alone." He sat his cup on the table. "*Jah*, I know we won't be able to eat a meal with our families or do business with them. But this is bigger than us. And besides, who says no to God?"

Eli threw his hands up in the air and walked to the window. "Not me."

Samuel added, "We can't turn back now. We know too much truth."

In the distance, Eli noticed lights flickering in the driveway from an incoming buggy. "What now?"

Rebecca moved to the window next to Eli. "Who could be out visiting in this weather?"

They watched as the enclosed buggy pulled into the barn. Eli headed to the front door and stepped out on the porch. Two figures moved across the yard, covered with a large black umbrella. The woman held a bundle close to her chest. Eli hollered over his shoulder. "Katie, it's your parents. It looks like they have Elizabeth with them."

Katie ran to the door. "Something must be wrong with the baby. Why else would they come out in this weather?"

Levi ushered Ruth and Elizabeth up the stairs and only stopped once they were out of the rain. Shaking the umbrella off, he leaned it up against the side of the house and followed Eli and Ruth inside.

Katie took Elizabeth from her mother's arms. "What's the matter?" She held the baby up to her cheek. "She doesn't feel warm."

Ruth wiped the rain from her hands and reached down to remove the blanket wrapped around the child. "Nothing is wrong with Elizabeth. But everything is wrong with this family."

Levi cleared his throat. "Ruth, take the girls in the kitchen. I'd like to talk to the boys for a few minutes."

Katie and Ruth headed to the kitchen, passing Henry and Samuel on their way.

Levi took off his hat and sat it on the bench near the door. "I think it's about time one of you explain to me the visit I had from Jacob just now."

Samuel pointed to the far end of the room and the rest of the men found a seat. Samuel followed and took a seat beside him. "What did Jacob say?"

"Word has it, you boys are holding secret meetings and evangelizing to the young folk in the community. Is that so?"

Samuel glanced around the room, looking for support. Henry spoke up. "It's true. Everything Jacob said and the rumors he heard are true."

Levi looked toward his son. Samuel grimaced. "I'm sure we've caused you concern. But it's what we've been called to do."

Levi raised his voice an octave. "You realize what this means, don't you?"

"*Jah.*"

"*Nee,* I don't think you do. You won't be able to work with me. It means your *mamm* won't get to watch after Elizabeth. And your *schwester* and Emma won't be able to work at the bakery. You will be cut off from your family." Without barely taking a breath, Levi looked at Henry. "And you! You're a minister, a leader in our community. God entrusted you. How could you even consider being a part of this?"

Henry took his hands and moved them up and down, hoping Levi would take the cue to lower his voice. The last thing they needed was for the womenfolk to get all worked up. "I think we should take this to the barn."

Daniel looked out the window. "The rain is coming down in sheets. How about the basement?"

Samuel didn't wait for an answer and stood and moved toward the basement door in the kitchen. Each man took his place behind Samuel and followed him downstairs. As they passed through the kitchen, each man found their wife's eyes and nodded reassurance in their direction.

Katie let out a deep sigh as the men's heavy feet met the wooden steps; Elizabeth started to fuss with her tension. Ruth moved to her daughter's side and took the child from her arms. "Now, don't be getting yourself all worked up. They will find a solution, I'm certain of it." She lifted the baby over her shoulder. "God's ways are always better than our own."

Katie glared at her mother's comment. "Do you know what Jacob said to *Datt*?"

In a sureness that had a way of calming Katie's fears, she replied, "I do. And it's an answer to my prayers."

Emma stepped up behind Ruth, brushed a wisp of hair from Elizabeth's forehead, and kissed it softly. "Answered prayer? How so?"

Ruth turned and patted Emma's arm. "It wasn't just you and Rebecca your *mamm* shared her truth with."

Rebecca stepped forward and asked, "You too?"

Ruth sat and balanced Elizabeth on her knee. "Your *mamm* and I were close. We got to spend a good bit of time alone near the end."

Emma leaned in and whispered, "So you know about the truth in Jesus?"

Ruth looked toward the open door of the basement and quietly replied, "I do, and so much more. I've been praying God would find a way to share the truth with Levi."

Katie's eyes misted over. "That would be a great answer. To know you and *Datt* could still be in Elizabeth's life is truly the perfect solution."

Ruth smiled and then answered, "God has a new agenda for all of us. That I'm sure of."

Maggie stood and walked to Ruth and laid her hand on her shoulder. "How long have you been waiting for God to answer this prayer?"

Ruth looked up at Maggie. "Five years."

Elizabeth rooted at her grandmother. Katie leaned over and took the baby from her arms. "You don't seem worried."

"Worrying only tells God we aren't trusting Him."

Rebecca shut the basement door softly and pulled a chair up next to Ruth, folded her arms on the table, and leaned in close. "But you've followed the *Ordnung* for all these years. You seem so satisfied with being an active member of this district."

Ruth crossed her legs and folded her hands around her knee. "On the outside, I may have looked comfortable, but on the inside, I was confused and scared. After your *mamm* shared what she learned from Mary, I started to question my own salvation. I needed to know the truth, so I went to Mary. She showed me where in the bible I could find my answers."

Emma took a seat across the table next to Maggie and asked, "Where did you find your truth?"

"The same place I assume you all found yours. In God's word."

Katie's eyes lightened and glowed. "You've read an English Bible?"

"Several times."

Maggie let her breath out slowly. "You've waited on God for five years. How have you not given up hope?"

Ruth's mind drifted for a few seconds before she answered. "I suppose God was preparing me. If He answered me right away, I might not have had time to study and be ready to serve Him properly."

Emma smiled and asked, "So Levi doesn't know?"

Ruth shook her head from side to side as her lips turned upward. "It's not my place to change his heart. That's God's job. All I could do was pray He would find a way to show him the truth. And look, here we are. I'm assuming the men are showing my Levi what you ladies already know."

Rebecca walked to the basement door and leaned her ear up close. "What if Levi chooses to ignore what Samuel might share with him?"

Ruth leaned back in her chair and replied with a sureness in her voice without hesitation. "Then I'll keep on praying."

Emma tapped on the table and looked at Ruth. "Do you think Mary shared the bible with any other women in the community?"

Ruth rested her elbow on the table and propped her chin up in her palm. "I wouldn't put it past her. She had more visitors than anyone else in the community. It wasn't uncommon to see two or three women a day stop by for a quick chat. As she put it, her kitchen was always open, and coffee was always warm."

Rebecca jumped away from the door as soon as she heard feet shuffle at the bottom of the stairs.

Levi opened the door and didn't stop as he headed toward the front door. "Ruth, come, we're leaving."

Katie reached up and took her mother's hand, feeling torn. Ruth leaned down and whispered in her ear. "I'm not worried, and neither should you be. God is bigger than all of this, I promise you."

Katie leaned her head against her mother's cheek and took in the warm embrace as she repeated her mother's words in her head. Holding onto her mother's hand until the distance between their fingers made it impossible. Her throat went hot and dry as she suppressed an internal sob.

Emma walked over to her best friend and wrapped her arm around her shoulders. The air in the kitchen left with Levi and Ruth, leaving all four couples struggling with Levi's abrupt departure.

Troubled, Katie looked across the room at her *bruder*. "So?"

Samuel shrugged his shoulders. "All we could do was pave the way. It's up to God to take it from here."

Katie was afraid of what life might look like if her parents couldn't be part of it. She looked around the room and started to cry. "Elizabeth won't know her grandparents. Isn't that upsetting to any of you?"

Daniel stooped down to her level and rested his hand on her knee. "Of course, it is. But you must understand that if we are asked to leave the church, it's because we're pursuing Christ. And He will never reject us."

Emma sat down beside Katie and ran her hand over the back of Elizabeth's head. "Don't you want Elizabeth to grow up knowing the true promises of God?"

"*Jah.*"

Samuel picked up his now cold cup of tea. "You know *Datt.* He has to think about things. He's not one to make any decision lightly."

Henry stepped beside Maggie. "We hit a nerve with him. I've seen that look before."

Maggie's eyes widened. "How so?"

"When years of instruction collide with God's Word, it doesn't line up and it leaves people questioning what they believe."

Rebecca started to clear the table. "So now what?"

Henry answered, "We're going to go help Ruth and Levi prepare for church tomorrow like we planned. Then we'll show up at church on Sunday like always and leave our fate in God's hands."

Eli carried a couple of cups to the sink. "Jesus never said it would be easy to follow Him."

***

Eli pulled his buggy up to the house and let Rebecca off before he pulled it up to the hitching line set in Levi's pasture. His starched black trousers, white shirt, and black vest clung to his skin. It was barely daybreak, and the humidity was already heavy in the air.

He unhitched his buggy horse and led him to the corral. Henry held the gate open and nodded. "Are you ready for this?"

"How did your meeting go with Bishop Weaver last night?"

"You'll soon find out. Here he comes now with Samuel and Daniel." Stopping short of the gate, Bishop Weaver motioned for Henry and Eli to join him at the side of the barn.

The bishop took his black hat off and held it by its brim, wasting no time getting to the point. "I suspect you all have thought hard and long about the consequences you face with going against the *Ordnung*?"

All four men shook their heads in unison.

"Then you leave me no choice other than to call you before the membership today."

Sweat trickled down Eli's brow and he let it fall to his chest.

"I suggest each of you let today's sermon settle in deep before you subject your family to the shame of excommunication." He nodded and left without letting any of them answer.

Only then did Eli take off his hat and wipe the moisture from his brow, following the bishop across the yard with his eyes. "We can't change the past. All we can do is move forward." He turned back toward his friends. "Who's in?"

All four men marched across the yard without a word and found their place in line behind the other men.

***

The warm sun did little to heat the chill Rebecca sensed when Wilma walked by. Her stepmother's lips formed a straight line as she tilted her head to the air as she passed. Rebecca whispered over her shoulder toward Emma. "I certainly won't miss her."

Emma pinched her side and whispered back. "Jesus instructs us to love all people, and that includes Wilma."

In a hushed tone, she replied, "But she grates on my every nerve."

"More reason to search your heart and fight against those kinds of thoughts. Remember we're to pray for our enemies."

308

Rebecca pulled her *schwester* close. "It's going to be a lifelong process for me."

Emma smiled then replied, "As it is with all of us."

Anna pushed herself between them. "What are you all whispering about?"

Emma hushed her. "Shhh … not now. We need to get inside; it's almost nine."

Anna's lip turned downward. "You two never include me in anything anymore."

Emma squeezed Anna's hand. "Soon, *schwester*, soon."

Anna grabbed Emma's arm and pulled her out of line. "What's going on?"

"I promise I'll explain later. But we have to get inside. We're in enough trouble today. I don't want being late added to our problems."

Anna reached out and pulled Rebecca close. "Please tell me what's going on. You're scaring me. *Datt* and Wilma whispered all morning, and I heard Samuel's name. Is he in trouble?"

Emma stepped out of line and moved to the side of the barn, letting the line of women file by. Emma tipped her head in closer to Anna and Rebecca stood guard if anyone got within earshot. "We don't have time to explain everything right now, but please know whatever happens today, we will find a way to see you and tell you everything we know."

Anna frowned. "I don't like this one bit."

Rebecca piped in. "We don't like keeping things from you, but there wasn't time. We promise we'll find a way to explain when the time is right."

The rueful look on Anna's face tugged at Emma's heart. How could she leave her *schwester* behind? She glanced over her shoulder and asked, "Do you trust us?"

Anna sighed softly. "Of course, I do."

"Then follow us today."

"What do you mean, follow you?"

Rebecca pulled them both back into line and whispered, "You'll see soon enough. Just step out in faith. Ignore everything you've been taught and follow us."

Anna's hand trembled under Rebecca's touch, and she brought her *schwester's* hand to cover her heart. "Do you see a change in me?"

"*Jah,* I do. I assumed it was because of Eli."

Rebecca's face changed to a pink hue. "Perhaps he had a little to do with it. But this heart change is God's doing and no one else's."

Rebecca ran her hand over her forehead just as they stepped back in line. "Please, Anna, trust us."

After adopting the solemn tone from the room, they found their place inside. Wilma turned in her seat two rows ahead and gave the girls a disapproving glare. It was uncommon to file in out of order of age, and the girl's tardiness showed heavily on their stepmother's face.

No matter how hard she tried, defensive anger welled up inside of Rebecca. She closed her eyes and asked God to remove the bitterness as she recalled Eli's words. *We can't store hostility in our hearts if we want to be one of God's messengers.*

She looked across the room until she found her husband. He, too, was seeking her. When their eyes met, the lines around his eyes softened. Little air was moving in the barn. But the thought of sitting still in the stifling heat left her more anxious as to what was to come.

The song leader sang the first word of the first song, and everyone joined in. The rhyming slow German song echoed off the barn rafters and made a wonderful noise.

The second song, the *Lob Lied,* also sang in German, would have prepared her heart for the upcoming sermon. But today, it did anything but settle her. The twenty-minute song lasted an eternity in Rebecca's mind, and it took all she had to concentrate on the words.

Thoughts raced through her mind as the habitual words flowed from her lips. *I don't even know what these words mean. For years, I've sung a song that has no meaning to me. Is this how God would want us to worship? Not knowing the meaning behind the songs that we throw up to the Lord each week.*

She took a few minutes to look down the row of young women all about her age. Their dark dresses matched the ceremonial expressions on their faces. Everything about Sunday morning had to be perfect, from the starch in their identical dresses to how many pleats were in their *kapps*. What did God care about starch or pleats?

Why hadn't she noticed it before? She followed the Old Order tradition for years because she was taught to do so. To value a work-based religion over God's actual word. But Eli showed her that her salvation was secure, all she had to do is believe in Jesus and no number of good deeds would pave her way to heaven. Let alone being discouraged from reading any bible but the German one. And that she didn't understand.

Never before had she wanted to scream from the rafters that they had it all wrong. She ached to tell the bench full of women that the only thing that mattered for their salvation was not how hard they worked and served, but by asking in faith for God to forgive them for their sins and ask Him to give them a new life in Jesus who died for them on the cross.

Her mind wandered while their lips moved along with the song. Did they see the change in her since she gave her life to Jesus?

She had to admit that she was even shocked at the radical change. Every passing day left her with a burning desire to share what she had learned. She was far from perfect, and she struggled with sinful thoughts each and every day. But now, she knew for sure her faith in Jesus would secure her eternity.

Oh, how she yearned to tell them that no matter how hard they tried, they would never be good enough to get to heaven without complete faith in Jesus Christ. But more importantly, she died to tell them that if God could forgive her for all she had done, He certainly would forgive them too. Who wouldn't want that kind of everlasting assurance?

Letting out a long sigh, she settled her eyes on the bishop and ministers who were coming into the room. Taking their seats at the front of the room, she silently prayed that the message would be something she could understand.

Her father was the first to speak, and he read scripture from a German Bible and took his seat. Next, Bishop Weaver preached on sin, and more than once, his words lingered on Samuel, Eli, Daniel, and Henry. She couldn't help but watch Eli's expression as the lines in his jaw struggled to stay still.

After the last minister stood to give his testimony and a recap of Bishop Weaver's sermon, the bishop stood and dismissed all non-baptized congregation members.

Rebecca sat between Emma and Anna. Quickly, she reached out and took their hands. Anna raised her eyebrows, looking for an explanation.

Bishop Weaver cleared his throat and stood silent for an alarming amount of time. Not a sound could be heard as he called all of them to the front of the room.

"I call the Samuel Yoders, Daniel Millers, Eli Brickers, and Henry Schrocks to the front of the room."

Anna let out a small gasp, covered her mouth with her other hand, and held tightly to Rebecca's fingers. Emma and Rebecca stood, and Rebecca bent down and whispered, "I promise you; it will work out perfectly." Reluctantly, Anna let go.

Rebecca, Emma, Katie, and Maggie moved to the front of the women's side while their husbands stood on the other.

314

Bishop Weaver waited until everyone was in place before asking them to drop to their knees. Rebecca looked toward Eli and waited for his lead. When he nodded his head in her direction, she complied and knelt, and everyone followed suit.

Rebecca held her breath. Not even a sparrow could be heard in the rafters above. It was as if the world stood still while they awaited their punishment.

Heads down and backs toward their community, Bishop Weaver spoke. "Our fellow brothers and sisters have gone against the rules of the *Ordnung*. Their sins are evangelizing and studying the English bible. Both require repentance before the church to stay in good standing with this district."

From behind, Rebecca heard a rustle of whispers. Bishop Weaver quickly quieted the room and continued.

"According to the rules set forth by our forefathers, any outward advances toward public evangelism are highly discouraged. All bible interpretation is through the Lord's appointed ministers and bishops only."

Walking in front of Henry, the bishop stopped and asked, "Henry Schrock, do you repent and promise to abide by the rules of this community, as well as forgoing participating in any public display of bible studies?"

In a show of disobedience according to the Amish church, Henry stood and confidently said, "*Nee.*"

Bishop Weaver continued down the line until he stood in front of Rebecca. All her friends answered the bishop's question in the same manner as she did.

The bishop asked the members to turn away. "As of this day forward, these eight members of our church will fall under the *bann*."

The room shuffled. Each side of the church turned away from the center of the room toward the wall, and he continued, "To stay in fellowship with this district, from this day forward until a public confession is made, no one will share a table, do business with, or speak to these eight members. If there should come a time when they request proper repentance, they will be accepted back into the church."

Rebecca lifted her head and steadied her eyes on her father. Only momentarily did he catch her eye and she noticed his chin quiver. She tore her gaze away and settled on Eli. His face, while under strain, brightened when she grabbed his eye. She saw nothing but complete assurance in his decision.

Samuel was the first to file down the center of the room. Each followed. Still, in total submission to Bishop Weaver's request to turn their back on the eight of them, Rebecca was shocked to hear Henry proclaim, "Jesus said, He who is not with Me is against Me."

Eli was next, as he added, "A house divided against itself will not stand."

Samuel stopped short of stepping outside and shouted. "If you want to know the promise of God. Follow us."

And as if on cue, Daniel added, "The Word of God is the truth to live by. We are leaving to pursue Jesus Christ."

As Rebecca and Emma reached the door, they heard Anna call their names. When they turned, Anna ran into their arms. "Please show me the truth."

Emma yelled in Samuel's direction. "God heard our prayers."

A line of their family and friends followed them out the door one after another; Levi and Ruth Yoder, Adam and Amanda Weaver, Teena and Lizzie Fisher, Joseph and Barbara Wagler, Ruben and Allie Miller, Bella Schrock, Edna Graber, and the Kauffman boys.

In awe of the scene unfolding, both Rebecca and Emma let out a joyous sigh and proclaimed, "Praise the Lord!"

Anna followed their voices and praised herself as their older *bruder,* Matthew and his wife Sarah, stepped outside into the light.

Rebecca walked toward Eli and let him wrap his arm around her shoulders. She leaned in and asked, "Now what?"

Henry overheard her question and was quick to answer. "Looks like we have the start of a new church. One where we can point people to Jesus through His word and let Him do the rest."

EPILOGUE

Rebecca took a seat on the ground between her mother's and Mary's small white wooden grave markers. Positioned under a large maple tree, Rebecca stretched her legs out in front and played with a pile of red and yellow leaves at her side.

Directing her words toward the small crosses, she began. "What a year it's been. I wish you both were here to see all the wonderful things happening in Willow Springs. Henry Schrock has taken the community by storm and led so many youths to Christ. God has definitely laid a hand on his leadership.

Datt and Wilma still want nothing to do with us, but that's okay. We're doing God's work, and we won't stop praying for them. Anna, on the other hand, is struggling with the separation. I, for one, love that she is living with us, especially since I'll need her help this winter when this little one comes along. Her heart is in the right place, but I fear her anxiety is getting worse with all the conflict with us leaving the church has caused.

Mamm, I wish you could tell me what I should do. *Datt* always said I sheltered her and didn't let her be herself because she always stayed in my shadow. I'm trying to get her to stand on her own, but she's becoming more of a recluse as the days go by. She attends church and bible studies with us regularly, but her mind is elsewhere. I just don't know what to do.

Mary, I can't thank you enough for showing me the way to God's forgiveness. And *Mamm,* your letter came at the perfect moment when I needed you the most.

I'm excited to tell you both I was finally able to track down the toddler's mother at the market and ask for her forgiveness.

God sure does have a way of turning evil into good. Little did I know at the time, but that small boy would go on to save three children at Pittsburgh's Children's Hospital who needed transplants.

Emma and Samuel still have not conceived another child. Still, in their wait, they're planning to serve as missionaries in Canada with Alvin and Lynette Miller from Ohio next spring.

Again, God stepped in and filled their days with purpose while he prepares the perfect time for them to grow their family.

Mary, you would be so proud. Emma's been teaching me all about gardening, and with her help, we've turned every bare spot in the yard back into the glory you once had. We even saved the patch of Johnny Jump-ups you were so fond of.

How can I thank you both enough for all you've done to etch away at my cold and lifeless heart? I'm confident I've tested God's patience more than once, but he's a loving God, and I know he forgives all. Even those times, I still struggle with what rolls off my tongue."

Stopping to rub her hand over the small bump across her middle, she continued, "I can only hope I'm half the woman the both of you have been. *Mamm,* I certainly didn't make your job easy. And Mary, you knew what I needed long before I knew myself. Thank you both for showing me the way to Christ."

Read more from ...

The Amish Women of Lawrence County Series
Anna's Amish Fears Revealed

Anna's

Amish Fears Revealed

THE AMISH WOMEN OF
LAWRENCE COUNTY SERIES - BOOK 3

Tracy Fredrychowski

PROLOGUE – BOOK 3

September - Willow Springs, Pennsylvania

A heaviness pressed down on Anna's chest, and she reached out to catch herself from falling. All morning her heart raced in anticipation of having to go to Shetler's Grocery. Rebecca continued to push her to get out of the house. But in all reality, she felt the safest tending to the chickens or helping with chores.

The grocery shelf shook under her weight. Before she had a chance to slip to the floor gracefully, her arm caught a stack of cans, making a commotion that could be heard throughout the store.

A fuzziness floated before her eyes, and she squeezed her eyes tight, praying it would pass quickly. An awful buzz echoed in her ears, and she leaned forward and put her head between her knees, and she prayed. *Please, Lord, make it go away.*

A tender voice and a warm hand on her back made her tip her head in the direction of the calming call.

"What is it, Anna? Are you ill?"

Even if she wanted to answer Mrs. Kauffman, she couldn't form two audible words if she wanted to. The older woman called out. "Simon, where are you?"

Did she hear correctly? Had Mrs. Kauffman just called for Simon? *Oh, please, Lord, not Simon. He can't see me like this.*

With a shuddering sigh, she tried to stand up, only to fall to her knees.

The older woman grabbed her arm. "No child, stay put. Simon is here. Let him help you."

It didn't take a second to know it was Simon just by the smell of pine on his shirt. His job at Mast Lumber Mill provided him with a steady job, even if he wasn't Amish any longer.

Their paths rarely crossed since he chose to follow his dream instead of his heart. But his touch only added to the sense of panic creeping through her skin.

Anguish filled her until she thought the weight would crush her lungs. Try as she might, she pulled her arm from his grip, but it only caused her knees to buckle under her. He placed his arm under her legs and around her waist and picked her up in one swift motion.

The sudden rush forced her head to drop into his chest. Without any option but to allow him to carry her, she stopped fighting and let his strong arms cradle her body.

"Relax, Annie, I've got you."

Annie, how dare he call me that. He lost that right four years ago. But she didn't have the strength to argue.

He stopped near the cash register and sat her down in the chair Mr. Shetler had pulled out. Simon snapped his head toward the direction of people who had followed the racket. "Someone get her a glass of water."

Simon fell to one knee, rested his hand under her arm, and whispered close to her face. "Did you have another panic attack?"

There weren't many people outside her immediate family who knew she suffered from constant panic attacks, and she'd hoped to keep it that way. When she lifted her face toward the crowd, her heart sank. Leaning into Simon's shoulder, she pleaded, "Please make them stop staring at me."

Simon lifted her from the chair and carried her outside while stating. "She's fine. Just a little overheated. A glass of water and she'll be good as new."

His mother followed them outside and opened the passenger side door of his truck. He gently placed her on the leather seat and thanked his mother.

Mrs. Kauffman leaned inside and handed Anna a cup of water. "Here, dear, drink this and let Simon turn on the air conditioner to cool you down."

She let her hand rest on her son's forearm. "I won't be but a few more minutes. Perhaps we should take her home?"

Tears blurred Anna's vision. "I've made a scene. I'm so sorry."

The older woman patted her arm. "Now, don't think another thing of it. These things happen."

Anna looked worried. "If Bishop Weaver catches you speaking to me, you'll get in trouble."

Mrs. Kauffman's tender tone calmed her fears. "You let me and Mr. Kauffman worry about Bishop Weaver. It will take more than this to ruffle my feathers."

Anna closed her eyes against the sudden tears and thought. *Why does this continue to happen to me?*

Simon closed the door, and she laid her head on the back of the seat. *Of all people, why did it have to be Simon?* That part of her heart had long closed.

She opened her eyes when Simon slid into the driver's seat and turned her head in his direction. If fear alone didn't paralyze her, the picture hanging from his rearview mirror made her gasp for air.

Without thinking twice, she fled from the truck and ran across the road and through the field that led back to Eli and Rebecca's.

Simon bellowed, "Annie ... please! Let me explain."

Read more of Anna's story in the third book of
The Amish Women of Lawrence County Series
Anna's Amish Fears Revealed

APPENDIX

Ginger Snap Cookies

Ingredients:

3/4 cup shortening

1 cup granulated sugar

1 egg

1/4 cup molasses

1 cup all-purpose flour

1 cup wheat flour

1/4 teaspoon salt

2 teaspoons baking soda

1 teaspoon ground cinnamon

1/2 teaspoon ground cloves

1 tablespoon ground ginger

Additional 1/2 cup sugar for dipping

Instructions:

- Preheat oven to 350°. Lightly grease cookie sheets.
- With a mixer, cream shortening and sugar until well blended. Add egg and molasses until combined.
- Mix flour, salt, baking soda, cinnamon, cloves, and ginger together in a separate bowl.

- Gradually add the dry ingredients to the mixing bowl at low speed until everything is incorporated and a dough forms.

- Using a small melon ball scoop, drop dough on prepared cookie sheets.

- Dip a glass bottom in sugar and lightly press each dough ball down.

- Bake for 8-10 minutes.

- Allow them to cool on a cookie sheet for a few minutes, then transfer to a cooling rack to cool completely.

WHAT DID YOU THINK?

First of all, thank you for purchasing The Amish Women of Lawrence County – Rebecca's Amish Heart Restored. I hope you will enjoy all the books in this series.

You could have picked any number of books to read, but you chose this book, and for that, I am incredibly grateful. I hope it added value and quality to your everyday life. If so, it would be nice to share this book with your friends and family on social media.

If you enjoyed this book and found some benefit in reading it, I'd like to hear from you and hope that you could take some time to post a review on Amazon. Your feedback and support will help me improve my writing craft for future projects.

If you loved visiting Willow Springs, I invite you to sign up for my private email list, where you'll get to explore more of the characters of this Amish Community.

Sign up at https://dl.bookfunnel.com/v9wmnj7kve and download the novella that starts this series, *The Amish Women of Lawrence County*.

GLOSSARY
Pennsylvania Dutch "Deutsch" Words

Ausbund. Amish songbook.

bruder. Brother

datt. Father or dad.

denki. "Thank You."

doddi. Grandfather.

doddi haus. A small house usually next to or attached to the main house.

jah. "Yes."

kapp. Covering or prayer cap.

kinner. Children.

mamm. Mother or mom.

mommi. Grandmother.

nee. "No."

Ordnung. Order or set of rules the Amish follow.

schwester. Sister.

singeon. Singing/youth gathering.

The Amish are a religious group typically referred to as Pennsylvania Dutch, Pennsylvania Germans, or Pennsylvania

333

Deutsch. They are descendants of early German immigrants to Pennsylvania, and their beliefs center around living a conservative lifestyle. They arrived between the late 1600s and the early 1800s to escape religious persecutions in Europe. They first settled in Pennsylvania with the promise of religious freedom by William Penn. Most Pennsylvania Dutch still speak a variation of their original German language as well as English.

ABOUT THE AUTHOR

Tracy Fredrychowski lives a life similar to the stories she writes. Striving to simplify her life, she often shares her simple living tips and ideas on her website and blog at https://tracyfredrychowski.com.

Growing up in rural northwestern Pennsylvania, country living was instilled in her from an early age. As a young woman, she was traumatized by the murder of a young Amish woman in her rural Pennsylvania community. She became dedicated to sharing stories of their simple existence. She inspires her readers to live God-centered lives through faith, family, and community. If you want to enjoy more of the Amish of Lawrence County, she invites you to join her on Facebook. There she shares her friend Jim Fisher's Amish photography, recipes, short stories, and an inside look at her favorite Amish community nestled in northwestern Pennsylvania, deep in Amish Country.

Facebook.com/tracyfredrychowskiauthor/

Facebook.com/groups/tracyfredrychowski/

Made in United States
Troutdale, OR
11/20/2023

14758961R00212